BE PREPARED . . .

Slocum undid the tarp, pried off the lid on the wooden explosives box and took out four of the waxed, red-paper-rolled cylinders. He wanted them loaded and ready. Carefully he used the jackknife from his pocket to open the folded, crimped end. Seated on the ground and listening to the horses breathe and stomp, he seated a primer attached to the cord deep in the black-powder granules, then repacked the end.

He had finished two of them when the kid returned.

"What's that for?"

"Fourth of July," he said, not looking up, busy with his task on the third one.

"It won't be that for six months."

"Then Chinese New Year." He affixed the cord and pressed the ends back. "Makes a good defensive weapon. Sometimes a little cannon can be a powerful instrument of war."

"You figuring on having that much trouble on this run?"

"Three dead drivers?" He cocked one eye into the sun and looked up at the boy. "This run ain't been no Sunday-school picnic . . ."

W9-ATZ-406

DON'T MISS THESE
ALL-ACTION WESTERN SERIES
FROM THE BERKLEY PUBLISHING GROUP

THE GUNSMITH by J. R. Roberts
Clint Adams was a legend among lawmen, outlaws, and ladies.
They called him . . . the Gunsmith.

LONGARM by Tabor Evans
The popular long-running series about U.S. Deputy Marshal
Long—his life, his loves, his fight for justice.

SLOCUM by Jake Logan
Today's longest-running action Western. John Slocum rides
a deadly trail of hot blood and cold steel.

BUSHWHACKERS by B. J. Lanagan
An action-packed series by the creators of Longarm! The
rousing adventures of the most brutal gang of cutthroats ever
assembled—Quantrill's Raiders.

DIAMONDBACK by Guy Brewer
Dex Yancey is Diamondback, a southern gentleman turned
con man when his brother cheats him out of the family for-
tune. Ladies love him. Gamblers hate him. But nobody pulls
one over on Dex . . .

WILDGUN by Jack Hanson
Will Barlow's continuing search for his daughter, kidnapped
by the Blackfeet Indians who slaughtered the rest of his family.

JAKE LOGAN

SLOCUM'S SIDEKICK

J

JOVE BOOKS, NEW YORK

If you purchased this book without a cover, you should be aware that this book is stolen property. It was reported as "unsold and destroyed" to the publisher and neither the author nor the publisher has received any payment for this "stripped book."

This is a work of fiction. Names, characters, places, and incidents are either the product of the author's imagination or are used fictitiously, and any resemblance to actual persons, living or dead, business establishments, events, or locales is entirely coincidental.

SLOCUM'S SIDEKICK

A Jove Book / published by arrangement with
the author

PRINTING HISTORY
Jove edition / May 2001

All rights reserved.
Copyright © 2001 by Penguin Putnam Inc.
This book, or parts thereof, may not be reproduced in
any form without permission.
For information address: The Berkley Publishing Group,
a division of Penguin Putnam Inc.,
375 Hudson Street, New York, New York 10014.

The Penguin Putnam Inc. World Wide Web site address is
http://www.penguinputnam.com

ISBN: 0-515-13056-7

A JOVE BOOK®
Jove Books are published by The Berkley Publishing Group,
a division of Penguin Putnam Inc.,
375 Hudson Street, New York, New York 10014.
JOVE and the "J" design
are trademarks belonging to Penguin Putnam Inc.

PRINTED IN THE UNITED STATES OF AMERICA

10 9 8 7 6 5 4 3 2 1

1

The big man sat behind the desk with his arms folded over his vest and leaned back in the swivel chair to consider Slocum. Ruff Glanding's dark eyes peered hard from beneath his salt-and-pepper eyebrows. Balding in the front, he combed his thin gray hair forward to cover the missing portion. His pale face reflected the light from the overhead lamp.

"So you're Slocum?" he asked in a big voice filled with authority.

With a calloused palm, Slocum wiped his whisker-bristled mouth. His temperament edged with impatience, he glared back at the man. "That's my name. Told you that."

"Well, I sent word to you three weeks ago to get over here."

"So?" He'd waited two days himself for Glanding's return from Sante Fe.

"I can't run a damn mail route, waiting three weeks for some ranny to show up to drive."

"I'm here now."

Glanding searched the top of his desk among the stacks of papers and receipts. At last, he found a piece of stationery and turned it toward the light filtering in from the dirty window to read it.

"Abe Sutter said you were tough—" Glanding looked up as if to measure the words on him.

"Abe ought to know." Slocum shifted his weight to the other boot heel with a clink of his spur rowel and folded his arms. This sumbitch hadn't even offered him a seat. He'd known men like Glanding before. They were hell on men and horses.

"Yes, Abe ought to know. But I need a driver to get the mail through to Prescott or I'll lose my contract. That make sense? I can't pay nothing unless the mail gets there."

"Far piece," Slocum said with a hunch of his tight shoulder muscles under the waist-length canvas jumper. He wondered if the man even realized how angry he grew, standing there like some schoolboy called on the spot by the teacher.

"I never said it was a piece of cake." Glanding scowled like he had been affronted by Slocum's complaint over the distance involved.

"Didn't ask you for one."

"Well, Slocum, are you tough enough that you can get the mail buckboard through and get back here each week?"

"I ain't failed at much I've set my mind to do."

"It pays twenty a week for the round-trip."

"I've got it figured where you need to pay me fifty a round."

Glanding's face grew red and threatened to swell to the point of explosion. He started to raise from his chair like a blown-up toad ready to leap. "Why, you ain't worth—"

"I ain't worth half that much, but the word's out that you ain't got a shipment through since you took over this contract. I don't make it through, then you don't pay me, but if I get there and back, I want paid fifty in cash after each trip."

"Go to hell! Why, you're crazy. I'd never pay that kind of money."

Slocum dropped his arms, rubbed his palms on the front of his waist overalls, and considered the blustery looking man. "I won't be in hell, but close to there. I'm spending the night at the wagon yard bunkhouse. You change your mind I'll be over there. Otherwise, I'll drift on." He turned and started for the door, disregarding the growing sheen on the man's face.

Glanding's boiling anger made no difference to him. Either his bluff worked for the higher pay or he went on. Only way to ever get anything out of a hard case like Glanding was to put the knife to him on the start; his kind of promises for advancement and future raises never materialized.

"Slocum!"

He stopped in the doorway and turned to mildly face the man. "Yes?"

"Pay you thirty-five and that's my best offer."

"Fifty. And it gets higher from here on." He managed a smug look for the red-faced man standing behind the desk.

"No one would pay that!"

"No one's got the mail through either." Slocum took his leave of the G and T Stage and Freight Lines office, smiling for the matronly woman receptionist, who stood up when he went past her desk.

He touched his hat brim for her. "Have a nice day, ma'am."

A rush of embarrassment flushed over her face, as if he had undressed her with his eyes. Anxiously, she glanced toward Glanding's office with a look that said that any minute she expected a bomb to burst in the place. Slocum gave her his best straight know-it-all grin and went out into the winter wind.

On the porch, in the harsh late afternoon, he fingered the few last coins in his pocket. Broke as a flitter. A man in his financial shape had a lot of nerve throwing a job offer like that away. A few flakes of dry snow swirled around in the air, and the cold chill soon found him.

Damn, it must be down near zero. He caught a glimpse of the great wall of red bluffs north of Fort Wingate. They sure didn't block much of the stiff wind that sought him before he reached the next porch's protection.

The saliva flooded his mouth as he considered the saloon's possibilities while he strode past it. A few good drinks of whiskey would chase out some of the deep chill in his bones. Damn, he could use lots of it. The audacity of that big buffoon offering him so little pay for such a tough task. Word was out all over town, the last three mail drivers were dead somewhere between here and the Arizona line. Whew, he could sure use something to drink. He closed his burning eyes to the enticing notion of a good slug of rye sliding down his throat.

He had barely enough money for a bowl of chili at the Mexican woman's place. Later he'd dig under his covers at the wagon yard and wait out Glanding's possible reconsideration. Come daylight, if he didn't get any word from the big man, he'd be forced to look for something else to do. He paused, shifted the .44 on his hip, shrugged the too-thin jumper over his goose-bump ridden shoulders, and with a shiver, crossed the street to Rosa's.

Inside the drafty cafe, the crackling fireplace drew him to the back of the room. He held out his hands to warm them on the radiant heat. The sand whipped up by the wind in the street gritted on his molars when he slid them over each other.

"Slocum?" Rosa said sharply from behind the counter. "You want some food, or are you going to use up all my heat?"

"A bowl of your spicy chili and some coffee," he said with a grin for the full-figured woman.

"You found some work?" she asked with concern in her voice.

He shook his head, unable to dismiss her worries. "He won't pay enough."

"Ho! Pay enough?" And she went off talking in Spanish about such stupid, proud men. He smiled after her car-

ryings on; two days he had known her and already she
had become his mother.

At last, warmed by the snapping hot fire off the juniper
logs, Slocum went and sat on a stool at the counter near
a boy in his teens, busy eating chili. Under a wide-
brimmed hat and longtail canvas coat, the youth looked
small.

"That Rosa is something." Slocum said, making conversation.

"Yes," the kid said in a soft voice.

Slocum glanced over. It was obvious to him that the
bulge on the boy's right hip was a Colt under his coat.
Must have run away from home. Hell, crazy kids did that
all the time. He had done that same stupid thing and could
tell the youngster a million reasons to go back; like he
never even tried to do it when he had the chance. Bull-
headed, maybe thickheaded was a better explanation. Him
and his old man could have made up—naw, they'd have
never made it without killing each other.

"They got any cheap rooms around here?" the Kid
asked, not looking at him and holding a spoonful of red
chili poised to eat it.

"Wagon yard costs a dime a night for a bunk." He
tossed his head to indicate the direction up the street.

The Kid nodded that he heard him and went back to
eating his food.

"Ain't fancy, but you won't freeze to death if you have
enough blankets of your own." Slocum looked up and saw
the buxom Rosa coming from the back. She set down his
steaming chili along with the big pottery mug of hot coffee.

"Ah, so what'll you do if you don't take the mail run?"
she asked with her hands on her hips. Well endowed, she
wore a man's shirt with the top two buttons open, exposing the deep brown cleavage of her breasts. A somewhat
older woman, Rosa, he imagined, must still be a barrel of
fun in bed. But the day before she had told him with a
curled lip that she had a man.

He stirred the spoon around the thick red mixture and

looked up at her. "I was looking for work when I rode in here."

"Yes, but there sure ain't much other work around here in the winter time. Be Christmas in a few weeks."

"Maybe get me a job working for old Saint Nick."

She laughed and looked enviously at him. "You Americans have so much good times then. When I was growing up, we always went to mass and acted solemn at Christmas."

"You've been missing all the fun. How many times you been married?" he asked, sampling the chili. It was fiery and would soon have his tongue seared. He reached for his coffee to settle some of the fire in his mouth and considered her plump body underneath the pleated skirt.

"Three times. Why, do you need a wife?" she asked suspiciously.

"For a night perhaps," he said, and then winked at her over the rim of the cup.

"No, I have a man, but I know one who would be that for a night—"

He waved her offer away. What she had in mind for him cost money. She didn't know how poor he in fact was.

"Maybe the Kid here would be interested in her," he said with a nod toward the silent one on his left.

The Kid's siege of coughing made Slocum turn to look at him. He would have sworn the boy was embarrassed and choked up by his words. Dang. Why, when he was that age—but not everyone had the same drive for the opposite sex.

"I'll . . . be fine," the Kid managed, waving their concerns away.

Slocum slowly savored his chili, making it last as long as possible. He watched the Kid pay out and leave under the bell that rang when the front door was opened or closed. He thought about telling him exactly where the wagon yard was located, but in this one-street town it wasn't hard to locate anything.

Rosa stood behind the counter and considered the wintery weather outside the front window. "More snow. Keeps my business away."

Slocum finished his coffee and agreed. Not much stirred in bitter weather like that. He set down the cup and looked at her. Her dark brown eyes met his for a long, heart-stopping moment.

"You are a dangerous man," she said under her breath and took up his dishes. For a long moment, she looked at the kitchen door, then at him as if she wanted to say something.

"You have lots of dishes back there to wash?" he asked, swinging his leg over the stool. Using a toothpick from the supply on the counter, he worked at his teeth and watched her start for the back. He followed her and stood in the doorway to the kitchen. Very intently, he studied her form bent working over the tub of soapy water.

He crossed the room until he stood behind her. "Need any help?"

She turned to face him and he tossed away the toothpick. A look of shock held her for a second, when she realized how close he was to her. He lowered his face toward hers, and she closed her eyes. His lips touched hers, and he felt her wet fingers on his cheeks. The fire of her kiss began to flair as her mouth opened under his. He drew her ripe body tight to his, imagining her naked. His hands ran over her backside, finally squeezing tight the half moons of her butt.

The doorbell rang, and she shrunk from him. Her hand flew to her mouth. "Out the back door," she hissed. "It may be Raphael, my husband."

"But I owe you—" he protested, wanting to pay her for the food as she pushed him outside.

"Go! Go quickly! You owe me nothing." Flushed-looking, she huffed for her breath and quickly closed the board door in his face.

In the cold, dark alley, flakes of dry snow swirled around him. He closed his jumper tight with his fist, licked his cracked lips to taste her again, and headed for the wagon yard. Damn, pretty heady kisser. He knew she would be salty if he ever—oh, well, he liked Latin women . . . even older ones. A deep ache in his crotch told him he would be paying for his indulgence. What the hell, he didn't have the job that he came all the way across New Mexico after . . . no money in his pockets and no female to share his blankets with on this bone-chilling night. Whew, his fortunes were lower than the belly of a side-winder in a sandy arroyo.

A few minutes later, he stepped inside the dimly lit bunk room that smelled heavy of sour socks and horse sweat. Under the yellow lamplight he saw three men with their hands in the sky. What the hell was happening? Then he noticed the white-faced kid from the cafe holding a sheriff's model Colt pointed at them.

"Hey, Kid, we was just kidding. You know, having a little fun is all," the big-gutted guy in the middle said. "We wasn't going to do nothing—"

"Well, you—you better keep your peckers in your pants or I'll shoot them off," the Kid threatened.

"You boys get a little rowdy with him?" Slocum asked, considering they must have tried or threatened to jump the boy and bugger him.

"We . . . were just fooling a little."

"Well, I say you need to get your gear and move out." Slocum gave them a sharp head toss. "I ain't going to sleep with my hand over my butt all night either."

"We were just kidding—"

"Get your gear and clear out," Slocum said, so there was no mistaking his meaning.

"You—" the big one threatened the Kid as he passed Slocum. "I'll show you what I can do." He exchanged a hard glance at Slocum, but kept picking up his things.

Slocum asked the big man, "What's your name?"

"Gill Doyle. We paid—"

"Go see the swamper, I don't give refunds. What's yours?" he asked the thinner man.

"Hardy. Who's asking?"

"Slocum's mine, and yours?" He pointed to the younger one.

"Everett Cone."

"Well Doyle, Hardy, and Cone, get the hell out and don't be slow or I'm filling your backsides full of lead!" His hand rested on the butt of his Colt and his eyelids narrowed to slits.

They scrambled to obey, catching their gear in both hands and bumping into each other to get out the door. Slocum shook his head in disgust at their final departure, then he went over and shoveled some coal into the pot-bellied stove. That task completed, he clapped his hands as if the whole thing was settled and studied the Kid. He appeared even younger than he had in the cafe. The boy uncocked the Colt and looked to holster it.

"Thanks," he swallowed hard. "They were acting pretty tough before you came in."

Slocum nodded, he heard him. "They won't be back. Take a top bunk. Shout if they do come back in during the night and try anything. I sleep light."

"Thanks again, Slocum. My name's Chris Patrick."

"Nice to meet you, Chris Patrick," he said, toeing off his boots and stripping off his pants to get ready for bed. In his longhandle underwear at last, he turned and saw the Kid was already in his upper berth and facing the wall.

Slocum gave a great sigh and climbed into his blankets in the lower bunk across the narrow room. He had waited two days for Glanding to get back from Sante Fe and that cheap dog only offered him twenty-five a week for his hell ride to *Preskitt*. What a waste of his time. He stared at the ropes overhead that strung the upper mattress and daydreamed of his brief kiss with Rosa. She sure tasted good. Been better if he'd had a shave and a bath before, but he couldn't afford either. He'd wager some money she could be fiery in bed, if he could only—he closed his eyes to go to sleep, trying to forget his still smoldering anger at that cheap Glanding.

He awoke in the night. The door was open and someone was coming inside. The lamp on the table was about out, but the arctic air rushed inside. What time was it? His fingers closed on the Colt under the covers with him.

"Slocum?" someone called out sharply.

"Yeah." He raised up and blinked. It was Glanding holding a candle lamp high and looking around. The big man was wrapped up in enough coats and scarves that if he fell down it would have taken a team of horses to pull him up. When Slocum threw his legs over the side of the bunk, he shook his head to dismiss the concern of the wide-eyed boy on the upper bunk across the way with his gun barrel pointed over the edge.

"Close that damn door, you're letting all the cold in here. What the hell do you want?" Slocum combed his too-long hair back with his fingers.

"Can you leave at dawn for Prescott?" Out of wind and sounding exhausted, Glanding finally dropped onto a straight-back chair. He began taking loose his scarf and clothing.

"You have changes of horses stationed along the way?" Slocum motioned with a head toss toward the west.

"Yes."

"They're broke?"

"Supposed to be."

"I don't have time to break horses and make that schedule."

Glanding nodded like he understood—waiting. Slocum rose from the bunk to near six feet in his stocking feet and stretched his arms over his head. Was colder than a witch's tit out there. "I want some money in advance to buy some things for myself."

"Go get what you want at the Jennings store, and I'll tell him to credit you."

"Give me a cigar," Slocum said and shook his head in disgust at the whole matter. They could have had all this settled hours ago. "Now tell me what got those other drivers killed."

"Hell, how should I know? One was robbed they think, the other, some renegade Injuns got him. One wandered off, must have lost his mind or went crazy."

"That's easy enough to do in this weather. I want a good greener and a Winchester in scabbards on that wagon's dash. Plenty of ammunition for them. A box of food and grain and a water barrel on that buckboard."

"Hell, I've got piles of mail—"

"Some of it can go next week. I ain't taking off out of here in a damn blizzard and not have supplies."

"All right." Glanding handed him a Havana cigar from an inside pocket. "Here."

Slocum ran his tongue along the brown cylinder. Tasting the fine tobacco, he decided, the cigar was good enough to eat. He bit off the end, spat it on the floor, and bent over to light the front end on the man's candle lamp. Then he drew on the rich smoke and sat back down on his bunk to savor the pleasure of it.

"I'll have the store open early so you can leave at four."

"You have that buckboard loaded and I'll be along." He gave the man a scowl. "It won't be no damn four o'clock, there ain't no such a time as that."

"Well, when then?"

"Gawdamnit, Glanding, I'll be there after I get a good night's sleep."

"Need a map?"

"It would help, and the locations . . . names of your relay people."

"I understand. And you get fifty dollars for each round-trip."

"I told you so a couple of hours ago." He looked at the man, pained as he began redressing. He felt so wrought up, he probably would never get back to sleep again. His last night for several in a warm bed, too.

"I'll have my part completed." The big man rose, looked across in the flickering light, started to speak, then, as if he saw the futility in it, began reclosing his outer clothes. "In the morning?"

"I'll be there."

Slocum shook his head in disbelief after Glanding went out. The swirling white stuff outside danced like fireflies on the gale force charging the hard-to-close door. He used his shoulder to relatch it. That cheap sumbitch would try something to cheat him and he knew it.

"Mister?"

He blinked in the dim light at the upper bunk where the boy was. "Yeah, Kid?"

"I'm going with you to Prescott."

"No, it ain't nothing for—" A cough cut Slocum off and he hacked over the cigar smoke until at last he managed to clear his throat.

"I can help. I ain't lazy."

"Hell, what in God's green earth do you want to go there for?" He put out the cigar to save the rest of it for the morning. No need to waste such an expensive smoke.

"They say there's gold at Prescott."

"Gold, mold. Kid, that is all rumors. I've been to a dozen of them places. The rich get the mines and the rest work like slaves."

"I've got to go with you."

"Hell," he shrugged. "It's your damn funeral. I'll wake you up before I leave and—" He waited for the boy to raise up in his bunk to say his final piece to him. "You can back out of going along any time. Hear me? Any time."

"I won't."

Probably won't either. Slocum recalled being that thick-headed. Dressed, he laid back down on the bunk. Crazy Glanding wanted him to leave at four A.M. Nuts to him. He closed his eyes, pulled up his covers, and slept.

Before daylight, the Kid and he took their breakfast at Rosa's. All Slocum could think about while rubbing the sharp whiskers fringing his mouth on his calloused fingertips was kissing her the night before. He watched the sway of her hips going up and down as she went behind the counter to wait on others.

"Where are you going now?" she asked, looking at him sharply, holding the coffee pot.

"Preskitt. I'm taking the mail."

"You're crazy, *hombre*. Why, they have killed all those men driving that mail buckboard."

"Hell, I finally got a job and now you don't like it."

His eyes met hers and he grinned. "You ain't worried about me, are you?"

"Crazy dumb gringo . . ." then she dropped her voice, as she finished refilling his mug. "You be careful, *hombre*. You come see me when you return."

He nodded he heard her, took the cup in both hands and blew the steam away. The Kid beside him had said little since he woke him. Hell, he dressed real fast, then went out and used the outhouse. Kind of a private sort of person. Slocum grinned to himself. Why he'd bet that poor boy thought his butt was had when them rowdies started in on him the night before.

"Chris, you ready to freeze your ass off?" he asked, then finished the last of his coffee.

"Yes." He nodded and reached in his pocket for money to pay her.

"Rosa, I'll be back in a week," Slocum said, counting out his last coins.

"If God looks after you," she mumbled and took his money.

"He will, you'll see," Slocum said, and then he grinned big. Damn, he would like to have her—she'd sure be a bedfull.

She made a quick gesture like a thrown kiss at him with her copper lips. That only made it worse. He rose, hitched the .44 on his hip, and led the way outside. They faced the sharp wind and the dry snow it bore.

"Wrapped up in blankets, we may not freeze to death," he said, and they entered the yard of the stage lines.

Slocum studied the two horses. They looked fresh and breathed vapor in great clouds. A stout looking pair of blacks. He checked over the harness as two Mexican hustlers wrapped in dirty blankets stood back. Chris waited. The sacks of mail were tarped down in the back of the buckboard.

"Get a few things at the store, then we'll pick up our own stuff at the wagon yard," he said to the Kid.

Glanding waved at him from the open office door.

"Better see what he wants." Slocum headed for the man.

"Here is that map, has all the relay stops and the names of the people to see at each one."

"There feed under that tarp for the horses?"

"You won't—"

"I may need it. I'll get some at the store. This weather ain't fit for a white man, and a damn Indian won't leave his tepee. I noticed you did put those two guns in the rig. I'll see you in a week."

"Slocum, I'm counting on you."

"You're paying for that."

"Too damn much."

Slocum ignored the man's complaint and stuffed the maps inside his shirt. The chill penetrated him fast. He was anxious to be under a blanket or two and on his way.

"Who's that kid?" Glanding frowned in disapproval.

"My swamper." Slocum said. "He ain't hurting a thing."

"Looks awfully young to me."

"We all looked like that once, a hundred years ago. I deliver this mail to the Prescott post office. I'll bring back what I can haul?"

"Yes, and get back quick as you can, we've got it piled up here. You need to make a one-week turn-around."

"Your other relay horses this good?" Slocum hooked a thumb toward the team.

"They're all that good or better. You should be all right." That said, Slocum left the big man. With Chris in the wagon beside him, he headed the team for the store.

Under the flickering candle lamps in the mercantile, Slocum checked over his supplies on the counter. "A sack of feed for the horses. Beef jerky, cheese, and hard tack to gnaw on." He had the clerk fill the small water barrel with fresh water. They'd be lucky if it didn't freeze tight outside. An extra woolen blanket lay on the counter. It was gray with a red stripe. He removed his hunting knife and had Chris hold the edges. Slocum cut a head hole out of the center and told the boy to put it on for a poncho.

"That'll shed some cold," he said and waved away the Kid's effort to pay for it. "We'll let Glanding buy it. Get me another one like it," he told the clerk.

When the man returned, Slocum did the same to it. Looking up, he asked, "You got any explosive blasting sticks? I mean black-powder ones." He removed his hat and put his poncho on.

"Got a case—but the better new stuff is—"

"Don't need that kind. A rough bounce of that buckboard out there and it might blow up. Give me some primer cord and a case of it."

A strange look crossed the Kid's face when the clerk went after it. "What're you going to do with that?"

Slocum smiled. "Pray that we don't ever have to use it."

2

He and the Kid left Fort Wingate, New Mexico Territory in the peachy light of the frigid December dawn. Slocum held the reins with the fresh horses moving out smartly on the main road. Plenty of freighters had laid over for the arctic weather to clear. Canvas-covered rigs lined the road. Their campfires' bitter smoke swirled in the air. Dry white feathers filled the ruts Slocum tried to avoid. He studied the red bluffs on his right and the mountains to the west.

His eyes seared by the sharp wind, and the unspoken Kid huddled in blankets beside him on the spring seat, Slocum headed for Arizona. Their first horse change would be forty miles west near the Arizona line. It was a damn poor time for him to have any regrets about taking on this mail run. He turned his face, cleared his throat, and spat the oyster off over the churning wheel. He should have bought a bottle of rye. It would have warmed his half-frozen innards anyway.

Mid morning, the sun finally shone through the broken overcast and tried without much result to warm the air. Fluffy clouds rolled by in between the solar efforts.

A few hours later, Slocum rested the horses in a deep canyon. He stepped off to relieve himself and he watched

17

the Kid head up the wash to be alone. That boy was simply a very private person. Slocum's own business completed, he undid the tarp, pried off the lid on the wooden explosive box with his skinning knife, and took out four of the waxed red paper-rolled cylinders. He wanted them loaded and ready. Carefully he used the jackknife from his pocket to open the folded crimped end. Seated on the ground and listening to the horses breathe and stomp, he seated a primer attached to the cord deep in the black powder granules, then repacked the end.

He had finished two of them when the Kid returned.

"What's that for?"

"Fourth of July," he said, not looking up, busy with his task on the third one.

"It won't be that for six months."

"Then Chinese New Year." He affixed the cord and pressed the ends back. "Makes a good defensive weapon. Sometimes when numbers are too great, a little cannon can be a powerful instrument of war."

"You figuring on having that much trouble on this run?"

"Three dead drivers?" He cocked one eyebrow and looked up at the boy. "This run ain't been no Sunday school picnic. Or had I neglected to mention that to you?"

"You said something—" The boy looked away.

Slocum shook his head and busied himself on the last one. "Maybe I didn't tell you straight enough."

"Never mind, I was going with you anyway."

"These cords are too long," he said, finishing the last one. "If you need a shorter one, I mean to make it go off quicker, you cut them down."

"I doubt I'll be using them."

"You might, if saving our butts depends on it."

"Oh, yeah, well, then I might. What kind of trouble're you expecting?"

"Robbers and renegade Injuns, Glanding said, that's who got them others."

"Who'd want to rob us? I mean, that sounds dumb. All we've got is mail." The Kid made a pained face and Slocum noticed his pale blue eyes. They were close to the color of silver.

It was time for them to get moving. Slocum rose to his feet and stretched, then he put the loaded sticks under the tarp beneath the seat. "There are lots of no-account trash out here that would rob a widow woman of her bible hoping to get some money for it."

"They sure must be desperate." The boy climbed onto the other side and took his place.

"Yeah, they're—desperados, is what they call them," Slocum said, deciding the temperature had climbed thirty degrees since they left Fort Wingate.

Once in their places on the spring seat, Slocum clucked to the team. At a long trot, they rolled across the grassy, juniper-studded land. They passed some empty hogans. The hexagon log structures with dirt piled high on the roof to shed water showed little sign of recent inhabitants.

"Navajos," he said absently.

"None around them, were there?" The boy twisted to look back.

"No, they're kinda superstitious. Someone dies in one they usually burn them. But if he died up in the Top of the World country they wouldn't come back and use it either."

"Top of the World country?"

"Yeah, they've got a mountain place where they go in the summer. Tall pines and cool lakes, that's their heaven." Up there sure didn't resemble this barren, short grassland with a smattering of junipers.

"You've been there?"

"Yeah, me and a Dine' woman shared some blankets once."

"Oh, I see," the boy said quietly, over the sounds of the horses' hooves and wheels.

"Wasn't a bad time either," Slocum said idly, remembering with fondness the nights in Lacey Blue's hogan. He couldn't recall at the moment why he finally left her; must have been the sugar foot in him that got to calling. If he had real bad faults, then his consuming restlessness might be his greatest. The urge to wander, see new horizons, like the one at the top of this grade. That itchy foot and the Fort Scott, Kansas wanted posters made him a tramp.

From the corner of his eye, he first noticed them. He spotted the multicolored ponies moving parallel to them in the distance. Black, brown, and white shapes filtered through the bushy junipers on a course similar to their own. He turned back, busy with driving his team on the long grade that stretched ahead of them. The animals could still give a good burst if needed. He wondered how many of them were out there. Perhaps a half-dozen bucks, maybe more.

He listened to the jingle of the harness, drum of hooves, and considered his next move. The riders were still too far away for him to decide a course of action. Were these the renegades that took out the other drivers or merely Indian men moving through the land? Before they reached the peak of this grade, he felt certain he would know the answer.

"You seen them?" he asked the boy.

"You talking about those paint horses?"

"And riders."

The boy nodded. "They going to give us trouble?"

"I ain't certain. They're kind of keeping their distance like they want to see who we are."

"What should we do?"

"Act unconcerned. If they don't mean any harm, we ain't got a thing to worry us. They mean harm, we'll give them some what-for."

"Simple enough."

Slocum told himself that before the day was over, he would see how the boy handled himself under fire. Those bucks out there weren't riding around for their health. More than likely they were renegades. The only thing the ones out there had was their own choice of times when and where to try something.

A red-tail hawk rode the stiff air currents and passed over them, his shrill cry like a warning. Slocum noted it and rose up to look off to the north for a sight of the riders. Nothing. He sat again.

"Some of them are south of us," the boy said, indicating to his left.

He never bothered to look, but studied the black horses' butts. "Then we can expect trouble; that ain't a coincidence."

They soon reached the crest without any trouble and headed across a vast mesa. The followers kept up with their progress, moving abreast of them, but keeping their distance far enough that Slocum could not make out their faces. By his count, he felt like there might be eight in total.

"What do you think they want?" the boy finally asked.

"Our clothes, the horses, the wagon even."

"They don't want the mail to read?" he asked with a grin.

"Hell, no. I'd bet there ain't a one of them red asses out there that can even read." Then he realized the boy jested with him.

"Mail'd make a heapin' big fire in a hogan," Chris said mockingly.

"Yeah," Slocum said with a chuckle. "Big fire. Maybe they're short on firewood."

"When will they attack us?" The boy dried his palms on the blanket over his legs.

"When the time is ripe."

"When is that?"

"Lord, Chris, if I knew that I'd be telling fortunes and getting rich."

Embarrassed, the boy turned away.

"Don't worry, it will take more than a half-dozen blanket-ass bucks to stop us."

"Yes, sir."

Several white-topped wagons showed ahead. Obviously some more freighters who were parked for the day. Trains had to stop and allow their stock to graze for several hours each day.

"Hello," Slocum said and reined up the team. A man in overalls walked out and greeted them. Several others rose up from their campfire to brush off their seats and came over to the buckboard.

"Having any problems?" Slocum asked.

"Naw, some bucks been hanging around."

"A half-dozen followed us in here." Slocum motioned to their back trail.

"We can go and flex out a few rifles," the man offered.

Slocum looked all around, but saw no sign of them. "Guess they're gone."

"You're welcome to stay with us."

"No, we've got mail to deliver."

"Be careful, mister," the man in the overalls said and waved good-bye as Slocum reined the team back toward the road.

No more sign of the bucks, still, an itch on the back of his neck bore a hole in him. Those bucks wouldn't give up that easy. They were too damn tenacious not to keep trying.

Elmo's place was a water hole under some spindly winter-bare cottonwoods. The trading post was made of logs and adobe and the front door stood open. A couple of hip-shot skinny paint ponies with closed eyes stood waiting at the hitch rack. A tall buck in an unblocked hat with eyes like an eagle stood near the doorway armed with a rifle.

"Hold the horses, Chris," he said and baled off. "I won't be long."

"Sure, sure," the boy said, taking the reins.

"*Yut-ta-hey.*" Slocum said to the guard in Navajo when he reached the porch.

The man smiled and babbled some more off in his own language at Slocum about how glad he was to see a white man who spoke the tongue. They exchanged a few more words of greeting, nodded cordially to each other, and Slocum went by him.

He entered the store and let his eyes adjust to the dim light inside. Several solemn-faced Indians squatted around the room. A white man in an apron came through a curtain from the back room to wait on him.

"Bottle of rye?" Slocum asked.

"Got some Yellowstone, but it ain't got any rye." He reached down and then set the whiskey on the counter.

"How much for the bottle?"

"Dollar and half."

"Wait." In disgust, realizing his finances, Slocum went outside to the buckboard.

"Chris, you have a dollar and half?"

"Sure, why?"

"I need a loan."

"Oh, okay." He raised up the hem of the blanket, scooted down in the seat, dug in his pocket, and soon produced the money in silver.

"I'll pay you back," Slocum said, taking it and heading back inside the post. The Kid waved away his concern.

"I've got some renegades trailed me the last few hours," Slocum said to the clerk as he paid the man. "Who are they?"

"Probably Dog Shit and his bunch."

"They tough?"

The man said something guttural in Navajo to the loafers. One of them replied, and the store keeper turned back to Slocum, who understood the buck's words. "He says they are now. They've got some ammunition."

"Ah-bliged." Slocum grasped the neck of the bottle in his fist.

He went out the door into the too-brilliant sunshine, and he blinked twice. On the ridge across the road and beyond the dry wash that paralleled it sat a half-dozen armed Indians on horseback. Spoiling for trouble.

"That Dog Shit out there with them?" he asked the Navajo guard, whose eyes were slits as he stood with the rifle ready in his hands.

"Hmm," he grunted and nodded.

"Good luck, my brother," Slocum said to the man. "But I think he wants me, not you."

Slocum didn't wait for an answer. He crossed to the buckboard and noticed the boy had the rifle ready in his hands with the reins.

"We may need this whiskey for snakebite. You ready for some action?" he asked Chris while he stowed the bottle inside of his bedroll so it didn't break and the whole time kept a wary eye on the bucks.

"They going to try us?" Chris asked, acting edgy. He set the rifle's butt down when Slocum climbed up.

"They look like they might," he answered. Seated back in place, he spat over the wheel and took the lines. Those bucks sure acted like they wanted their hides.

Ready to roll, Slocum clucked to the team. They must be better than halfway to their first relay station. Close to mid-afternoon sun time anyway. He swung the team of blacks toward the road and put them in a hard trot. It would be a long day with those renegades dogging their tracks, but he had the bottle of whiskey to look forward to. He stretched the tight muscles in his back and took a new seat on the boards. Quite a spell till dark, and the Navajo back at the traders had said, they had ammo.

Like smoke on the wind, the Indians vanished again. Slocum still purposely took their next break on a wind-swept rise where there could be no surprise charge. They chewed on jerky and washed it down with the icy barrel water. No sign of the Indians, but Slocum knew they were out there. Somewhere.

The warmth of the sun increased and caused Slocum to regret not getting more sleep. No sign of the bucks, which meant to him they were either planning to attempt a holdup or had given up. He gave odds on their planning to rob them. So far no one to his knowledge had made it to the Arizona line with the mail. It must be three or four hours ahead. All the daylight that was left.

"Maggard's ranch is the place where our fresh horses should be waiting," he said, speaking out loud for the boy's sake. "I asked that guy back there who it was trailing us. Said the leader's name was Dog Shit."

"That's his real name?" Chris asked, squatting on the ground beside him.

"Real enough. Also said that this Dog Shit had ammunition."

"Will we be to this Maggard's ranch before dark?"

"For our own safety we better be."

"And if we ain't—"

"We'll keep pushing."

"How close you want them before I need to light and throw the blasting sticks at them?"

Slocum smiled with pride at the boy's words. "Close enough. You know, you and I may make us a team yet. Load up, we need to get on to Arizona."

3

Slocum raced his tired horses toward the fast-falling sun. The red ball in the west would soon tuck itself under the horizon. They needed to find Maggard's ranch before night closed in on them.

He saw the weathered slab board sign etched with the Maggard name and an arrow nailed to a post. Feeling better, he shared a nod of approval with the boy and reined the horses northward with little in sight but the vast rolling brown grassland. They soon topped a rise and he spotted the corrals and low-walled buildings. Relief spread through him despite the falling temperature and low light spreading over the bloodred-bathed land.

"We didn't find this too soon," the boy said, sounding relieved and looking back over his shoulder.

A pack of dogs charged out at them when they neared the place. Yapping and barking, the curs surrounded the rig as Slocum reined in the team and let the jaded horses walk the final hundred yards. A big man with a bushy beard stepped out from the low-eaved log house with a dirt roof. Hatless, he carried a Winchester in his right hand.

"Glanding sent us," Slocum said over the bark of the dogs.

"Shut up! Get the hell out of here." The man began to swear and kicked the dogs away, his boot sending the closest one yelping in pain and fear. "You must be the mail driver?"

"Yes, I'm Slocum. This is Chris."

"Pearcy's my name." He nodded to the boy.

"You Maggard?" Slocum asked.

"Nope, I work for him. He's gone somewhere. We've been expecting someone for two months. Turned them damn horse loose when no one came."

"You mean you don't have Glandings' horses up?" Slocum stared in disbelief at this half-witted dummy. The fresh horses weren't there. Weren't ready. He tried to fathom the truth, not believing the situation it left him and the boy in.

The man shook his head indignantly. "Hell, no one ever come for them. Figured he'd gone broke."

Slocum inhaled deeply for control. "They around? The horses, I mean."

"Somewheres." Pearcy shrugged his shoulders. "I've got some food ready, come in. Too damn dark to look for them now."

Slocum shared a head shake with the boy, who indicated that he was going off to relieve himself.

"Where's he off to?" Pearcy asked.

"I guess to relieve himself."

"Hell, I just piss off the porch. Ain't no one here but us."

"Come on, I need to wash up. He'll find the way," Slocum said to take the man's mind off the boy's private ways. Still disturbed by Pearcy turning the horses out, he tried to dismiss the matter. They might catch them in the morning, but they wouldn't be shod or in any condition for the grueling day ahead.

"What do you know about this Indian Dog Shit?" Slocum asked when the man poured him steaming water in the tin basin on the log bench table outside the front door.

"He's a rascal. Maggard once caught him stealing his traps and beat him half to death."

"Well, he's got ammunition now, they told me." Slocum lathered his hands with the soap and began to wonder about the tired horses. "Don't you have any horse hustlers here to rub down the team and care for them?"

"Me."

"We'll turn them loose after we eat," Slocum said, disgusted with Glanding's arrangements. If they were all like this setup, he'd never get to Preskitt in a month.

The boy returned and joined them.

"Wash up. We'll unharness the horses after we eat," he said to him and went inside.

Pearcy served them stew. The meat was stringy, and Slocum never bothered to ask him the source. The canned tomatoes, rice, and beans in it were palatable enough, the coffee strong. The three ate in silence for a long time.

"That Dog Shit's got how many bucks with him?" Pearcy finally asked.

"I'd say a half dozen," Slocum speculated over a spoonful of food.

The boy agreed with a nod to that number.

"He's come up in the damn world. Them mostly boys riding with him?" Pearcy asked as if thinking about their numbers.

"Never got that close to them. They tracked us most of the day."

"We seen them at that trading post," Chris said, not looking up.

"Yeah," Slocum agreed. "But I couldn't age them very good at that distance. When's Maggard due back?"

"Damned if I know. He wanders all over. Looks for gold, traps, trades."

Slocum nodded. If all of Glanding's stage stops were this poorly run, him and the Kid would be damn lucky to ever get there and back.

"You're welcome to any bunk," Pearcy said, indicating the ones around the walls of the room. "I always sleep on the floor."

Slocum agreed. Full of the stew, he sat back and considered all they must do before bedtime. "You have a lantern to use while we unharness?"

"No."

"We better get busy, Chris. It'll be pitch dark out there in a few minutes," Slocum said, and the two hurried outside.

They quickly stripped the harnesses off and led the pair to a tank for water. Satisfied the horses were cool enough to safely drink and not colic, Slocum let them take their fill.

"Ain't this his job?" Chris asked in a quiet voice.

"He's letting us do it. Smart enough, ain't he?"

"Yeah," he whispered back as his horse let the water roll out of his open mouth before going back for more.

"We better," Slocum cleared his throat and raised his voice, wondering why they were whispering to each other. "Find his grain, feed and put them in the corral, we'll need them in the morning. Those others won't be in any shape to drive all day. We don't have any choice but to let them rest and stay here all night."

"I can't believe he turned them others out. Wasn't old what's-his-name paying him?"

"You mean Glanding? I suppose he was. They made a deal, but no one showed up in the past month, so he figured the deal was off."

The boy shook his head, and they led the team to the corral in the last of the twilight.

"You boys got them took care of?" Pearcy shouted from the doorway.

"Get two pails of grain for them," Slocum shouted.

"Ain't got none left. When no one came, I fed it all to that shoat we just butchered."

"I'll get some from the wagon," the boy said quickly and hurried after the sack, while Slocum sought control of his temper.

"How many horses did Glanding leave here?" Slocum asked when the man came over picking his teeth.

"Four."

"How much feed?"

"All that a damn shoat could eat in a month. Oh, we fed the horses some for a while, then when no one come we figured the deal was off."

"You and Maggard figured the deal was off?"

"Didn't take no genius to do that. Them mail wagons never came by here. I wasn't tending them horses for nothing and feeding them good feed that would lard up a shoat. They could earn their keep outside, like the rest of the stock does. Ain't hurt them a bit."

"When did you see these horses last?"

"A week or so back."

"What I figured. Now, you get them horses up, shoe them, and feed them grain. I'll be back here with that buckboard in five days and if you ain't got them horses ready and fed up, I'll—I'll—" He let his voice trail off. "You'll wish you had."

"Ain't any reason to get upset. If you'd come by like he said, I'd a had 'em ready."

Slocum grasped the man's shirt front in his fists and jerked his face inches from his own. "I'll beat the living pea wad out of you if it isn't done right by then. Hear me?"

"No need to get upset—sure, sure, I'll have them ready."

"I've got them fed," the boy reported, packing the rest of the grain sack on his shoulder. The boy's words jarred him enough that Slocum let go of Pearcy, who staggered back from him.

"Good. Thanks, Chris." Slocum headed for the house, afraid he might beat Pearcy to death if he stood out there much longer. One thing for certain, he hadn't charged Glanding enough, not near enough for the way this job turned out to be.

At the frosty crack of sunup with the blacks in harness, Slocum swung out on the road from Maggard's lane and headed west. No sign of the renegades, but he wondered if they stayed clear of Maggard's place fearing the man from the past. No telling. According to Glanding's map, him and the Kid were headed west for the Little Colorado River and the next change of horses.

How well they got along depended on how well these horses could hold out for the next relay station. Grain-fed, he hoped they maintained their stamina. This would be another long day by his calculations, they needed to make more miles to even turn the mail around in a week. That meant Glanding needed more fresh horses at relays along the way and less shiftless contractors like Pearcy. He shook his head to dismiss his contempt for the lummox.

They were well down the road in midmorning when he reined up to rest the team on a rise. A cold draft of sharp air swept across the barren tabletops.

The Kid jumped down and went off behind a juniper and returned. He stretched his arms skyward under his blanket coat. "How many more days to get there?"

"At this rate, four more." Slocum shook his head in disapproval.

"Hey, we're getting company!" The boy shot to his tiptoes to better see them. By then the sounds of the renegades' thundering horses became clear.

"Get in the wagon." Slocum grabbed the Winchester and, seeing the Kid had his handgun out, spoke to him. "Don't use it until they get in range."

Yelping and making dust in their wake, several renegade Indians were coming at them on their paints. He could make them out, hatless, waving their long guns and giving cries that even above the growing wind sounded fierce. Carefully aiming, he fired, and the bullet rose a puff of dust close to the leader. It sent his horse sideways and upset his rider so that he clung to the horse's neck to save himself from falling off.

The entire incident was enough to cause the attackers to draw up. Slocum bounded on the seat, took the reins, and nodded to the Kid. They headed west in a hard run.

"They're still coming after us," the Kid said with a serious look on his smooth face.

"Yes, I know. Reach under the seat and get out some

of those Chinese firecrackers. New Year's Eve just arrived." Slocum half turned to see the individual bucks had become more enthused again about chasing them. With his free hand, Slocum reached out to steady Chris as he went under the seat after the explosives. In an instant, he was back up on the bench holding the four red sticks.

"How long a fuse?" Chris asked, swaying back and forth with Slocum as the buckboard lurched around on the dry ruts.

"Use a long one first. It may go off behind them and scare the pea wadding out of them." A quick check over his shoulder of the charging bucks filled Slocum with a new urgency, and he used the lines to set the team into a harder lope.

Flush-faced, Chris quickly agreed. A stick of it locked between his knees, he fought to light a match and not fall off the seat. With one arm Slocum grasped the boy's shoulders to hold him steady as they were both jostled around on the seat by the wagon's rough actions. Two matches struck—nothing. Finally, the boy's small hand cupped a match long enough to start the cord sizzling.

"You have plenty of time," Slocum assurred him, seeing the light of fear in the boy's blue eyes. "But toss it in the road behind us, so it will be right in their path when they come."

Apprehensive looking, the boy turned around on his knees, steadied himself with one hand on the seat back, and gave the stick a hard fling. Slocum quickly glanced back, satisfied they were clear of it. The six or so warriors were coming hard. This trick had to work. He turned back to the front and urged the team on faster. Hunched over, he cringed and waited for the blast.

The Kid watched their back trail, clinging with his elbow over the seat back. The yelping and war cries grew closer. Then the thunderous boom and the Kid gave a shrill scream. The blacks tucked their tails at the blast and lurched forward even faster. Slocum drove his bootheels into the dash to brace himself. He needed to stop the startled team before they ran away and wrecked the rig. With all the muscles in his shoulders and arms, he sawed on their bits to slow them down.

"We got 'em!" Chris shouted, and pounded him on the shoulder.

Slocum could only look back at the large cloud of dust and see his Plan A had taken out several riders and scattered the rest. He closed his eyes for a second in respect to the powers that be as the team slowed to a trot.

"We did it, Slocum! We did it!" the boy shouted, his face flush with the excitement.

That was only round one and Slocum knew it. Sometimes all one did by shooting a bear was arouse it more by wounding it. Only time would tell their plan's effectiveness. He closed his eyes; this damn job would be a lot more work than even he figured.

"You've done that before," Chris shouted, bouncing on the spring seat. His blue eyes danced with the excitement.

Slocum nodded. It wasn't over yet. Just one incident of many, to his way of thinking. When and where would Dog Shit try to attack them the next time? He drew the horses down to a jog. Be another long day.

4

They didn't see Dog Shit or his followers the rest of the afternoon. Slocum noted how impressed Chris had become since the blasting stick trick. He acted much different. It had changed him from a quiet Kid who acted like his shadow might bite him to an open and enthused individual.

"Who has our horses up here?" Chris asked, motioning toward the west.

"A trading post, it said on the papers. Run by a man called Markam."

"You reckon he fed his hogs with Glanding's grain too?"

"Lord only knows, but I'll be a mad son of a buck if he has."

"We can't be that unlucky twice." Chris made a face at the mares' tails in the sky. "You read weather?"

"Got an old friend called Charlie, he says those kind of high, thin clouds mean moisture's coming."

"That would mean snow?" The boy drew his blanket closer. "Hasn't warmed up much today either."

"I know. Not since they tried us, anyway."

"Whew, I was sure nervous lighting that fuse. Wondered if it would blow up in my lap."

"Blasting sticks are never a joking matter, but a little cannon never hurt winning a war none."

"You fight in the war?"

"Yeah, everyone fought."

"North or South?"

"Don't matter now." Slocum used the lines to make the tiring blacks trot faster.

"Why not?"

"It's all over and like a bad scab, no need to pick at it. Where did you run away from?"

"St Louis."

Slocum let some time pass, but the boy said no more about his roots. He said that much, anyway. Maybe later, the Kid would tell more about his past. He had some good upbringing, probably an education. When no more story came forth, Slocum studied the distant purple mountains in the south and wondered when the Navajo renegades would return.

"You from Texas?" the Kid asked in a small voice.

"Been there. I was raised in Alabama."

"You must have fought for the Confederacy."

"I did, but like I said, that's all over."

"My daddy was with General Sterling Price. You ever meet Price?"

Slocum shook his head. "I heard about him."

"He talked about him a lot."

"Your daddy still alive?"

"No," the Kid said and glanced away. "Is yours?"

Slocum wet his lips and stared ahead. "Not now."

"I see."

"I came home from the war thinking I was a man," Slocum said, recalling the past. "I wasn't. The home place was in shambles, he'd lost about everything. Him and I fought all the time. Maw said that was because we both were so much alike. When she died, we fought worse, like we blamed each other for her death."

"What did she die from?"

"I'm not sure, she took sick one day. We never figured

it was anything too serious on the start, but in a few days, she slipped away."

"You and him fought more?"

"Yeah. I rode out one morning and he ran out of the house, shouted after me, 'Don't you ever come back.' "

"Should you have gone back?"

Slocum turned in the seat and looked hard in the boy's blue eyes. "I never doubted it a day, until now." He paused and considered the matter, then he clucked with a slap of the lines for the team to pick up their trot.

The Kid folded his arms over his flat stomach like he was deep in thought and slumped down in the spring seat.

"See those cottonwoods ahead?" Slocum turned toward him, and the boy nodded. "That means water too. It should be the Little Colorado River. We may be close to the next relay station."

Chris looked over his shoulder and then turned back, obviously seeing nothing. "Good."

Markam's Trading Post hummed with Navajos, both large and small. Numerous wagons and thin horses in harnesses stood hip-shot about on the hard-packed, bare dirt lot that ran from the river to the well-built building that housed the sprawling structure and pens. A large warehouse behind looked secure and the trade was brisk going in and out of the open doors when Slocum reined up in front of the wooden platform that served as the porch.

"*Buenos tardes*," a Mexican man said with a slight bow. In his ears, silver earrings sparkled in the late afternoon sun.

"Good afternoon to you too," Slocum said as he wrapped up the reins. "Do you have fresh horses here for Mr. Glanding?"

The man blinked his brown eyes in disbelief. "We thought he was dead."

"No, two days ago he was as alive in Fort Wingate as I am. Do you have fresh horses for me?" Slocum knew there wasn't another hard day left in the grunting and dust-snorting blacks. They had done their part well, but they needed fresh horses to continue.

"Yes, I will have someone get you fresh horses—"

"Not until morning." Slocum had made up his mind that they both needed some sleep. The threat of those rengades attacking them again out there made him shy from the notion of pushing on in the night. He turned to the man. "That's U.S. Mail on here. Can you keep it safe until then?"

"Of course, I am Pasquel, señor—"

"I'm Slocum. This here is Chris. We've had a helluva long day."

"This way." Pasquel motioned them toward the door, then told an Indian youth to put up the horses and wagon. "He is an excellent employee. He will take good care of the horses, your things, and the mail and have fresh ones ready for you in the morning."

"Is Señor Markam here?"

"No, he is in Sante Fe getting supplies. We have had so much business, we are low on stocks and he went to arrange for them."

Pasquel showed them to a table and chairs. A Mexican woman soon brought them hot coffee, and Pasquel returned with a bottle of red wine. The Kid wrinkled his nose at it, so Slocum poured himself a glass. He nodded his approval when Pasquel asked to be excused to handle other business.

"I completely forgot about the whiskey," he said aloud to the Kid after tasting the wine. He set his cup down and tried to recall the day. Chased by Indians, had tough jerky for lunch—his nose began to tingle at the alluring smell of roasted beef. The same woman soon delivered them bowls of beans, a platter of flame-blackened beef strips, and a stack of corn tortillas.

With a cup of coffee cradled in his hands, Chris said, "Wow, this sure beats Pearcy's stew. What do you reckon was in that stew last night?"

With some beef wrapped inside a still-hot tortilla in his hand, Slocum looked hard at him. "Dog meat."

"Oh no. . . ." The Kid's face paled and he looked sick.

"Hell, you ate it already and ain't dead. Dig in, boy. This here's real good food."

"Oh, Slocum, that is so bad." He made a pained face at him and shook his head.

"This ain't. You better dig in before it gets cold."

Chris dropped his gaze to the plate and began to pick at his food.

"Better eat. This maybe our last real meal until we reach *Preskitt*."

"You keep calling it *Preskitt*. Others call it Prescott. Which is it?"

"They ain't never been there. Folks up there call it *Preskitt* and if you don't want to be branded as a green horn, don't call it Prescott. That's another place on this earth."

"This is good," the boy finally agreed, eating with more gusto.

"There is a room in back," the woman told them, "ready for you two to sleep in."

"*Gracias*. This food is *mucho bueno*," Slocum bragged on her.

She beamed and hurried off. He decided everyone worked hard at this post. The store still bustled with trading under the flickering candle lamps hanging overhead. Markam had himself a rich business.

Slocum took out the map and read the instructions. Twenty miles west, there would be more fresh horses the next day at the McNeal place where the territorial road turned south for some sixty miles to join General Crook's road. Supposed to be two more relay stops before Camp Verde and the final sixty miles to Preskitt.

Slocum sipped the wine slowlike and spoke his thoughts out loud to the boy. "We've made close to eighty miles today, that's around a hundred and forty so far. It's that far again to Preskitt by this map. That means four days going and four days going back, which means we can't make this run in a week."

"What are you planning on doing?"

"Next time, we're cutting that time down."

"How?"

"Get fresh horses at Pearcy's and go further the first day. When the moon's out, drive at night. But I figured it would be safer to wait till sunup to try the next stretch."

"You're the boss. This warm store's sure making me sleepy." Chris stretched and yawned big.

"So is this wine," Slocum said and refilled his cup with the last of it. "No need for any to go to waste."

A commotion broke out in the store portion and Slocum rose with the cup of wine in his hand. In a moment, Pasquel came with a small billy club and struck the obviously noisy drunk over the head. Store workers unceremoniously dragged the stunned hell-raiser out onto the porch.

"No problem, a drunk is all," the man assured them.

Slocum nodded and downed his wine. He set the cup back on the table.

"You really think that dumb Pearcy fed us dog meat?" Chris asked before he stood up.

"Yeah. After supper I never used the outhouse like you did, I just went out the back door to pee. He had some fresh hides nailed on the wall back there. One was brown, one was black."

"What's he doing with dog hides?"

"They make women's slippers out of them. Fancy shoes. Ain't you ever heard of putting on the dog?"

"Yeah, I've heard of that a lot, but I never knew it meant they were made of dog hide."

"They sure are." He threw open the door to the room the woman had indicated for them. The two beds were already outfitted with their bedrolls from the wagon.

"Great service here," Slocum said, undoing his gun belt.

"Yeah, sure beats that dog-killer's place. Why, I bet he had body lice in his place."

"What's so bad about them? I knew Indians picked' em off regularly and ate them."

"Oh." the boy said with a shudder of revulsion. "Slocum, I may never sleep again."

"Close your eyes, it ain't far behind them if you're as tired as I am." Standing stocking-footed in his long handle underwear and turning back the covers he had rolled out on the bunk, he considered the day. He and that boy hadn't done bad, but they needed to go faster. It was a week's run and they *had* to make it in seven days.

5

Dawn formed a purple seam when they took to the spring seat. Their breath making clouds of vapor, the matched bays in harness acted eager to go. Slocum waved to Pasquel and the stable boy when he swung the rig around and headed west.

"Maybe we can have a day of peace, Christopher," he said, with a wide, pleased grin.

"Yeah," the Kid agreed with a faint look of something wrong.

Slocum dismissed it. The boy had obviously seen more in the past few days than before in his life. He'd damn sure seen a lot more desert. The team stepped lively, and Slocum was forced to hold them back. Did that worthless Navajo renegade Dog Shit lie in wait somewhere west? Only time would tell, and they had three sticks loaded, and ready, in case he did try something again.

They passed several wagon loads of Navajo families, going to Markam's, no doubt. The man drove, and the woman used the whip to keep the usually mismatched horses trotting. Some of them grinned and waved, others solemnly nodded.

The juniper bushes dotted the land, and several flocks of Indian sheep out grazing threw up their heads to watch

43

the passing mail rig. Slocum rested the team on top of a grade. The sun warming them some, they drank cold water from the barrel and sucked on peppermint hard candy the Kid bought at Markam's.

"What're you going to do at Preskitt?" Slocum asked.

The Kid made a pained face. "I need to be honest with you."

"Oh?" Slocum said, seated cross-legged on the dry grass. He glanced up at the boy's back. His slender shoulders hunched under the canvas coat and he looked off to the distant purple mountains in the south.

"Yeah, there's some guys out to kill me."

"Ha, ain't no more than have the like in mind for me. Who are they?"

"I don't know their names. One's redheaded and has a scar on his left cheek, and the other one wears a patch."

"Why they so all fired up about killing you?"

The Kid turned and looked pale. "They murdered a deputy U.S. marshal. Stabbed him to death. I saw them do it."

"They know you seen them?"

"Yeah, they chased me for blocks. I barely got away."

Slocum nodded. Serious enough business, witnessing a murder of a law man. "You figure they're still looking for you?"

"Yes. That's why I had to go to Preskitt with you."

"Where did you last see them?"

"Dodge City, Kansas."

"How did you get to Fort Wingate?"

"Caught a freighter headed west out of there before they saw me."

"Why didn't you go on with him, the freighter, I mean?"

The Kid didn't answer for a long while, then he half turned and spoke over his shoulder. "I had my reasons."

"Good enough," Slocum said, getting to his feet and brushing the grass and dirt off the seat of his pants. "This afternoon, you better learn how to drive these ponies. Get up there."

"Yes, sir!" A grin of pride crossed his face and he bolted aboard.

"Don't 'yes sir' me," Slocum said and swatted him on the seat of the pants with his palm. "You need to learn how to drive away from them fellows looking for you."

Slocum climbed up and for a minute, he would have sworn he had embarrassed the boy with his friendly slap. His face looked a little red but it might be wind-burnt. Eyes straight ahead, the Kid had the reins, and when Slocum found his seat, he drove them away.

At noon they stopped along the banks of the Little Colorado and ate jerky. A red-winged blackbird called loudly, clinging tenuously to a wind-waving willow. When the shadow of a low-flying hawk went over them, Slocum, busy chewing, threw his head back to see it.

"Who's at the next stop?" the Kid asked.

"It has the name K. McNeal written in, supposed to be a ranch. The ranch brand is an MK on the sign, according to his notes. You know Glanding never said much about anything, except he didn't want to pay anything for the run."

The Kid nodded. "Guess he had no takers when he came after you."

"I got lucky."

"Wish I had your experience at handling men like him."

"It'll come with age."

"I hope so," the Kid said and downed his tin cup of water. "You want me to drive some more?"

"Might as well. You've done damn well so far." Slocum brushed his hands off, prepared to drain his bladder, and undid his pants. "I'll be ready to go in a minute here." He undid his pants, stared off to the north, and pissed with his back to the rig and the strong wind.

Finished, he shook it off and put it away. "Ready to go. Damned if I don't think the clouds are getting thicker in the west."

The Kid agreed with a nod, busy acting ready with his driving; he clucked to the bays. They moved out smartly. Settled back, Slocum studied the narrow stream of the

Little Colorado beside the road. The brown-stained flow dodged sand bars and moved over ripples.

"Kinda nice not to have any crazy Indians after us today," the Kid said.

Slocum glanced at their back trail, then agreed. "It sure does make it better. I could halfway like this job, you doing the driving and me riding shotgun."

"Suits me."

Midafternoon, they discovered the MK sign, and the Kid turned the horse up the lane. Slocum felt good they had made so much progress. The pole corrals and the low-walled house loomed ahead in a grove of cottonwoods. A couple of black and white stock dogs came out to bark at them.

A woman in her forties came out. Buxom and square shouldered, she gave them a wary look and held a Winchester by the gun barrel in her left hand.

"I'm looking for K. McNeal."

"That's me," she said, in a gravel voice; all the time suspicion masked her face. "I suppose you finally got here with that mail?"

"We've got mail for Preskitt. They never said nothing about your mail." Slocum stepped off the wagon and bent to pet one of the dogs.

"I don't have none coming. But I knowed who you was when I seen you coming. Hell, did it take a month to get here?"

"Been some serious problems. They've killed a few of the drivers. Chris and I are the first ones to get this far."

"I can see that. My name's Kay. Well, get your asses off the wagon, I've got fresh horses in the pen for you two. I'd a gawdamn sure had them harnessed, but I give up when no one came by here."

"We can do that," Slocum said.

"He ain't dry behind the ears yet, is he?" she asked openly.

"Chris? He'll do."

"Your boy?"

"No, ma'am. We're friends."

She shrugged and headed with Slocum for the corral. "You two must be tough as nails to get here, if'n they took out three of them drivers."

"We've had some trouble."

"Solved it, huh?" She looked Slocum over like one would a horse to buy. "Hell, you look tough enough."

"I guess."

"I wouldn't guess. I'd bet that's why old Glanding hired you." She rubbed her long fingers over her mouth as if still appraising him. "Hell, if you get real horny sometime," she checked to be sure the boy was far enough away on the wagon not to hear her and dropped her voice. "Why you could share my soogans some night."

"That's a plumb generous offer," Slocum said. "I may just do that some time, Kay, but me and the Kid need to make some time up this trip."

"Yeah, but you damn sure won't regret it," she said privately.

"Never figured I would," he said, and looked at the slick-coated wagon horses eating hay. "You did well by his old ponies. They look in great shape."

"They are, but not for where you two are going."

Slocum turned and frowned at her.

"Can't you see that storm out there? It's been building all day. Too warm." She shook her head in disapproval. "It'll come in here and dump snow up to a tall Indian's asshole."

"We head south here for the rim, right?"

"Yeah, Issac Denton's got your next change at the Diamond D. He'll have you fresh horses, but you'll be damn lucky to ever make it there."

Slocum turned and looked at the Kid coming to join them. "Kay says she thinks that storm coming in will stop us from getting through."

"Whatever you think." The Kid shrugged off any concern.

"I think we better change teams and head south, make it as far as we can tonight."

"Fine."

"Well for crying out loud, I can't tell which one of you two is dumber," Kay said, and shook her head in defeat.

"We're on a seven-day turn-around on this mail run, we can't afford any more delays."

"Well, you two hardheaded peckers get that harness off, we can have your leather asses gone from here in ten minutes."

Slocum grinned at her words. She set her thin lips in a smug curl. When the boy climbed on the buckboard to drive it over to the corral, she finally said to Slocum out of the side of her mouth, "Don't you forget, that offer's good."

"Kay, I won't," Slocum promised, considering the ripe body under the calico dress with canvas men's jeans underneath it.

She winked at him and grinned. "Didn't figure you would."

They changed harness to the two stocking-legged sorrels. She ran to the house to get them some food to eat while they made the switch.

"Whew, she's tough as any man," the Kid said, looking toward the cabin to be certain they were alone.

"Half alligator and half bear. You ever made love to one?"

"No," the Kid said quietly.

"Hell, you have to wear spurs to bed to even stay on them. They buck and growl and even bite."

"Oh."

"Yeah, but they can be more fun to screw than the fanciest dove that costs twenty dollars."

"I see."

"Oh," Slocum said with a shrug and ducked under the horse's head to adjust the other side. "In time you will." He straightened, took off his hat, and wiped his gritty forehead on his sleeve. It would be a long night ahead for them.

Kay was on her way back with food. Slocum's stomach felt close to his backbone. The rising cloud bank had grayed out the sun. Only a few hours of daylight left, then it would be dark out there before they found Denton's place.

"This Denton's. How far south?"

"Twenty miles, I guess," she said, handing each of them a plate of meat, tomatoes, and rice.

"Can we find his gate in the dark?"

"Yeah, he's got a big rail over it on posts. An archway, you know."

Slocum nodded, sampling the food. "Damn good."

"I'll be ready when you come back. How long will you be getting back?"

"We better be here in three days."

"Aw hell, you'll never make that schedule."

"We have to," Slocum said, before taking a bite of the browned slab of cold steak in his hand.

"You two will be froze stiff out there in a snow drift. Damn shame too."

"How's that?" Slocum asked, between hurried bites.

"'Cause you two are the best-looking studs been by here in ages." Then she threw back her head and laughed out loud.

Slocum said with his mouthful, "Me and Chris'll be back."

"I ain't so damn certain. That's a real storm heading in here." She rubbed a hand over her hip as if to scrub away the hurt. "My bones been complaining since yesterday."

"Have those fresh horses ready for us in three days," he said. He handed her the empty plate, gave her a kiss on the leather-tanned cheek, and stepped onto the wagon. Chris, already on the seat, gave her his plate and thanks, too.

"You're damned fools! I told you so," she shouted as a fresh wallop of wind swept up dust and grit in their faces.

"See ya!" Slocum shouted, and clucked to the fresh horses. They left her yard in a dead run. When they reached the main road he wheeled the buckboard around in a high fan of dirt. He was half off the seat, his boots braced on the dashboard, handling the team and shouting, "Hang on boy, we're making up some time!"

6

The snow began to fall. In the last hours of the dim afternoon, the wet flakes melted on his face leaving small drops of cold moisture in their place. He spoke to the fresh horses, keeping them in a long trot. The bare ground began to take on a veil of white as the rhythmic clop of the horses' hooves struck the hard-packed road surface and the ring of the iron wagon rims' song became a symphony to them.

"You ain't said much the last few miles." Slocum elbowed the Kid.

"Yeah, we've got this snow, and how we're going to find this next ranch is on my mind."

"Gets too bad we'll den up till daylight under the wagon."

"But, I mean how will we see? The sun'll go down soon and there won't be any light."

"Guess we'll have to trust the horses."

"What if they can't see and go off a bluff?"

"Ain't too likely." He reached up with the top of a knuckle and rubbed the itch on the right side of his nose.

"It ain't worrying you one bit, is it?" The Kid looked over at him with a question written on his face.

"To be real honest, no. What I've got in mind is to deliver this damn mail and get back."

"You need the money?"

"I'm broke enough. I borrowed money off of you to buy that bottle of whiskey I haven't even touched," he said, thinking how he'd forgotten it until that very moment. "Why, are you rich?"

"No!" The Kid shook his head emphatically, then looked up at him. "Will you make another run?"

"Maybe—"

When Slocum glanced over at him, the Kid simply nodded, all huddled under the blanket poncho and hat pulled down by a chin string. Small stars of white began to stick on the crown of it. Slocum turned back to the road, lined with some low brush and black sage. He clucked to the horses and slapped them with the reins to keep up the pace. It would be a long night.

The white mantle on the high tablelands made it lighter outside in the night. Slocum guessed the time to be near midnight. He blinked and elbowed the Kid. "Ain't that a ranch gate?"

"Looks like it," the Kid said, and yawned and stretched. "You reckon that's Denton's?"

"If it ain't, they're having company anyway," Slocum said and reined the team in under the crossbar.

In a quarter mile, dogs began to bark. The dark outline of corrals and several low buildings appeared. At last a light came on in a small window as Slocum pulled up at the front door.

"This Denton's place?" Slocum shouted.

A whiskered man in a knee-length night shirt over his longhandles came out holding up a candle lamp. "Yeah, who's asking?"

"I need some fresh horses."

"Why, I'd gave up on you acomin'. Get inside here. Too damn cold to palaver out there."

Slocum nodded to the Kid, who quickly dismounted and shot off to go around the building.

"Who's he?" Denton asked, pushing down his bushy mustache with the web of his hand.

"My helper had to go, I guess." Slocum hitched the team to the rail. "He'll be back. In fact, I need to go, too."

"Piss right there," Denton said, "Ain't no women folks here. Then come on in."

"We will."

"Lord," Denton said, shaking his head. "How long has it been? First one was due here over a month ago. I figured the mail deal was off when no one ever came."

"You still have the horses?" Slocum asked, concerned standing beside the wagon wheel as he let loose a long stream into the several inches of snow on the ground.

"Sure, but I was thinking they just never got the business off the ground."

"Well, he lost the first three rigs and then couldn't find a driver."

The Kid returned, nodded to Denton, and went past him inside. Slocum finished his pissing, shook it good and put it back. Then he joined Denton and they went inside the ranch house.

The Kid was warming his hands at the fireplace. Slocum realized how good the heat would feel to his numb fingers. He joined the boy and studied the licking flames.

"We made it this far," Slocum said.

"Yeah, I sure never thought we would."

Slocum nodded. "Some things in life are real challenges."

"Real ones," the Kid quickly agreed.

"I've got some food," Denton offered.

"That's fine, but tell you what, I could use about four hours sleep better right now after we put the horses up," Slocum said, deciding that if he ate he might not sleep. "What about you, Kid?"

"Sleep sounds great to me," he said with a shake of his head, looking around the room for a place to do it.

"Let's unharness and we can do that," Slocum said.

"Yeah, unharness," the Kid said numblike, and stumbled for the door. Slocum and Denton both laughed at him.

The horses were cared for and their bedrolls spread on the floor. Slocum fell asleep when his head hit the blanket.

Denton's rattling coffee pot and stoking the fire awoke him. How long had he slept? Not near long enough, but the only way they'd ever make the schedule was to push on.

"I got some bad news for you," Denton said. "That rim road ahead of you could be belly-deep in snow. You may not make it through there. Ain't been anyone but three guys gone by here headed that way two days ago."

"Who were they?"

"Big guy named Doyle, some old man, and a young guy named Everett with him."

"The Kid knows them." Slocum, seated on his blankets, tossed his head and pulled on his boot.

"Hmm," the Kid snuffed out his nose, fighting to get his own foot gear on. "I met them before."

"Kind of hard cases to me," Denton said, "But you get all kinds coming through here. They needed to fix a shoe. I let them. What did they want from you?"

"Tell him, Kid," Slocum said, standing up and stomping on his boots.

"They got pretty rowdy."

"They were fixing to bugger him in the bunk house at the wagon yard, but he got the drop on them," Slocum said.

"You should have used your gun on them," Denton said with an angry scowl on his face.

"I thought about shooting them," the Kid mumbled and excused himself to go outdoors.

When he closed the door behind himself, Denton nodded to Slocum. "He's not got a lot of seasoning, has he?"

"He's pretty gritty though. Them bastards claimed they was only funning, but I believe they were serious."

"Sonsabitches, I'd never let them used my smithing stuff if I'd known they were that perverted."

"They headed for Preskitt?"

"I guess, that's where the road goes. You figure they'll try something like that again? They asked about the wagon horses too. At the time I figured it was plain curiousity. You reckon it was?"

"Don't know," Slocum said, considering the matter.

"I'll have some antelope steaks ready here in a few minutes, got some rice and peppers and some left-over biscuits. How will that be?"

"Grand fare," Slocum said. "Which ones are the horses? I'll go hitch them while you get the food ready. We need to make some tracks."

"It's a solid black gelding and black mare with a star that matches; the rest are my saddle horses."

"Good, we should be back in two days. Grain the ones we drove in well."

"I'll have them ready for you."

"Thanks," Slocum said, meeting the Kid at the door and explaining his plans to hitch up. They joined forces and soon had the blacks hooked to the wagon with the first light of predawn on the white land. Slocum mentioned Doyle's inquiry about Glanding's horses to the Kid.

"You reckon Doyle's laying for us out there?" the Kid asked, with a concerned set to his face looking over the backs of the horses at Slocum.

"He ain't no grizzly bear."

The Kid dropped his gaze and shook his head in defeat. "That's all you're afraid of?"

"I respect them," Slocum said and motioned to the cabin. "Denton's got food ready for us. Let's go eat it."

They were on the road in twenty minutes. An orange seam cut the horizon filtered by clouds, and flakes swirled about them. The harness jingled and the blacks took a good long trot, churning up pads of compact snow from inside their shoes and throwing them off with each upturned step.

"You know Doyle before that night?" Slocum asked, his eyes narrowed and studying the distant range. His mind was more on the road conditions ahead than the question.

"Sort of. They were with the wagon train I took out from Dodge City."

"They tried that before?" He frowned over at him.

When the Kid didn't answer, he glanced in that direction again. Maybe he didn't want to say. Slocum felt a growing rage building inside. That was why the Kid had used his gun, he knew what they'd try to do to him. Worthless bunch. The notion made him madder.

The Kid turned and looked him square in the face. "They knew who I was."

"Who are you?" he asked, busy looking at the road and the butts of the blacks.

"My real name's not Chris, it's Sarah Christine. People call me Christine."

"Whew!" Slocum let out a deep exhale. He looked at the gray ceiling of wooly clouds that stretched for an eternity. *He was a girl.* Damn, how many times in the past three days had he whipped his old pecker out and took a leak like they were all alone in a strickly male world.

"That makes lots of difference," he said, and a cold shiver ran up his spine.

"I was desperate. Those two men that killed that marshal, they would have killed me. So I left St. Louis and took the train to Dodge dressed as a boy. I'd cut my hair. In Dodge, still running scared, I took a ride with a freighter like I said. On the way, he discovered I was a girl and well, it was either submit to him or walk." She didn't look up at Slocum, but stared straight ahead. "I didn't mean to lie to you."

"I understand. How did Doyle figure in?"

"The freighter was a guy called Murphy, Jock Murphy. He must have told him about me being a girl. Murphy was a pig, a slob. I don't know how else they found out. Maybe they figured it out." She shook her head. "I don't know. Anyway, I quit Murphy at Sante Fe, got away, and found me a ride to Fort Wingate. Then that night, Doyle and them showed up and discovered me in the bunkhouse before you came in."

"I'm sorry," Slocum said, at a loss for words.

"I'm not a damn whore."

"Never said you were."

She reached over and clapped him on the leg. "You remind me of Vince Winston."

"Who was he?"

"The man I lived with before all this happened. We weren't married, but that wasn't here nor there. I ran away from home in Illinois when I was fourteen, met Winston, and we became a couple. That was six years ago. These are his clothes, we wore the same size. After he was murdered, I ran off. That night I circled back to our place, got some of his clothes, our money, which wasn't much, and his extra gun."

Slocum clucked to the team as they started up a rise. Then he turned back to her. "You left home at fourteen."

"Yeah, my stepfather couldn't keep his hands off me."

Slocum nodded. "Sorry about you losing the man in your life."

"Vince Winston was a real one," she said.

Slocum glanced over and saw her shoulders were shaking under the blanket poncho. She was crying. He shifted the reins to his left hand and put his arm over her shoulders.

"Christine, I figure you've got a couple of them cries coming."

She looked up with her wet lashes, red eyes, and shook her head. "It just wasn't fair, Slocum. Just wasn't fair."

He hugged her thin shoulders tight. "Life's like that, girl. Life's really like that a lot."

7

The snow grew deeper, the junipers taller as they gained altitude. Snow-mantled pinions began to appear in groves. The blacks were making good time in the four inches of white stuff. Slocum only wondered how far they could go before the depth made their way impossible.

"Where is the next relay stop?" she asked, then blew her nose in a white kerchief.

"A place called Thorpe's, but it's over the rim."

"You still going to act like I'm a boy?" she asked, sounding concerned.

"Sure," he agreed.

She hugged his arm. "You won't regret it. I'll pay you back."

"Don't worry about that," he said. "We get to the top of this grade, I aim to rest the team and vent some of Denton's coffee, girl or no girl along."

"Don't you do one thing different," she said and then shook her head. "I'm sure glad I was able to tell you."

"Yeah, you didn't know me that well on the start."

She squinted her eyes and looked away. "Yeah, a girl that lost her virginity to her own stepfather at thirteen. . . . Well, I ain't an angel. But outside of Winston, there have been some real sorry men in my life."

Slocum drew the blacks to a stop. "Well, here is the palace of snow where we're stopping at for a few minutes to let these blacks catch their breath." He tied off the reins and jumped down.

Not as cold as he expected, and sunlight showed in shafts peering through the cloud cover. He went about ten yards and with his back to the wagon, he peed. A damn girl. He should have guessed. When he finished and turned back she had returned from her trip behind some junipers.

"How deep will the snow get, do you think?" she asked, squinting against the blinding glare and looking to the south.

"Deep enough," he said, and they mounted up. By midday they reached the Mogollon Rim, and a fresh, cold wind from the south swept their faces. The snow-covered, pine-clad mountains stretched before them.

The road made a Y and they took the right fork in the unmarked snow. A white-capped board sign pointed with an arrow *Preskott, ninety miles.* Another one mentioned Camp Verde. He wondered about the accuracy of the distance, but soon dismissed it. They were headed west again. The road soon took on steeper proportions and he was forced to hold back the team, both up- and downhill. It slowed their pace.

The depth of the drifts increased. Then they pulled over a ridge and the narrow road ahead lie tucked close to the mountainside like a shelf. He hauled up the horses, then he stood up to better see the way.

"It sure ain't very wide, is it?" she asked, peering over to look down into the bottomless canyon on his side.

"I'm going to walk ahead, since there aren't any tracks. You drive them."

"What if—"

"Stay on the right side of the wagon seat. If it goes over the edge, you jump off your side."

"Damn, Slocum, don't you ever worry about anything?"

"More serious things than that, yes." He handed her the

reins and climbed off. His slick leather soles skidded on the slush and he almost went down. With a look over his shoulder at the long way down, he decided to better watch his footing.

"Bring them easy," he said, once out in front of the team.

"What if they can't stop?" she asked in a high-pitched voice.

He looked back and gave her a wry shake of his head. "Bail off then."

"Oh," she huffed.

The blacks followed Slocum going downhill. He descended faster in places on the slick soles than he wanted. Ocasionally he turned to nod his approval to her driving. From time to time, the blacks lost their footing, but they were making it with her white knuckles holding them back.

The ledge road clung to the side of the mountain, but it soon made a serious turn ahead and disappeared. Slocum hurried to get out of the animals' way. Could she control them—too late to do anything else, he made longer strides.

"Hold them back," he said, turning to see her standing with her feet braced, fighting the reins.

"I'm trying, I'm trying."

"Good," he said and slipped. It drew a sharp, "oh, no," from her. Only a drift of wet snow stopped his going downhill. At a depth that came to his knees, he wondered about the horses, but had to regain his footing and hurry on. They were coming, ready or not.

The deeper snow gave her a chance to hold them back some. Slocum touched the sheer face of the mountain with his hand to keep his footing. Helluva road, if you called it that. Then he rounded the bend, out of breath and halfway skiing on his soles, wondering about her and the team. He found a boulder top to brace off of and saw the bobbing heads of the proud blacks coming, then the ashen-faced girl holding back on the reins.

She would do it.

A half hour later they reached the bottom, and she leaped off the wagon, raced over and hugged him. "Oh, I was so scared coming off up there."

The sun had come out and in the canyon the heat had begun to rise. Droplets of water dripped off the conifer needles.

"You did great." Grateful and relieved to be off the mountain, he held her tight and looked down into her blue eyes. The moment lasted for a long while. She closed her eyes, turned up her small mouth. He kissed her, his lips on her cold ones, which soon began to warm.

"Do we have time to celebrate?" she asked when their mouths had separated.

"Whiskey?" he asked, holding her tight to him.

"I really thought . . . well—" She looked around. "Is there any place here to put down a bedroll?"

"Be kinda cold," he teased her, figuring out her intentions, which appealed to him.

"No, it won't be for long," she said and twisted away. In a second, she fetched one from the wagon and was unfurling a canvas ground cloth. She paused to look at him.

"Get your boots off," she said with a frown.

"Yes, ma'am," he said and grinned big in anticipation.

Seated on his butt on the blankets, he pulled off his wet boots with some strain. He looked up as she shed the poncho and set it on the edge of the buckboard. In his stocking feet, they stood side by side, undoing their pants. The race to undress became a contest. In a flash, they were naked as Adam and Eve and slipped quickly under the blankets.

"Whew, it wasn't that warm," she said and slipped into his arms.

He had only a glance of her small pear-shaped breasts, topped with knot-sized pink nipples. Their mouths met and his calloused hands raced over her velvet skin. Warmth from their bodies captured by the soogans quickly warmed them. The impatience of her kiss began to arouse him. Her fingers soon closed around his growing shaft and she gave a gasp.

While she squirmed to get underneath him, the covers fell off his shoulders, exposing his bare back to the cool air. No time to worry about being cold. The consuming urgency made him ache to drive his manhood into her. Her legs parted, and the aching head probed her gates. Then he began to drive it in deeper. The muscles in her stomach tightened, and she issued a groan of pleasure as she fought to meet his charge.

Then their lovemaking grew more intense. Once, she tried to cover him with the blankets, but the fury of their actions made that impossible. Her hands drew his waist down hard on her flat belly and her heels pressed on the backs of his knees. She launched herself harder and harder at him. Her spasmatic contractions soon began to trap his manhood and they both strained in and out of each other. Their breaths' fury soon became a swoon song. Then in an explosive conclusion, they collapsed in a spent pile.

Slocum shut his eyes, too weak, barely able to hold himself up from crushing her. She cupped his face and kissed him with a renewed smile.

"We need to rest them horses more often," she said pertly.

"Yeah," he agreed.

8

At the lower elevation, the snow had begun to melt faster. The harness jingled and the wagon rims cut through the slush to the rocks with a new ring. The trotting horses soon splashed slop on them. Slocum could see the Verde Valley below them as they dropped off the rim. The sun, low in the west, made purple streaks on the last bands of cloud stretched across the clearing sky.

He glanced over at Chris. Her hat set on the back of her head, the speed of the team curled the brim back. With a knowing smile, she reached over and playfully squeezed his leg. He winked at her and hoped they'd make Thorpe's before dark. Then they had the last sixty miles to make it to Prescott, according to Glanding's note.

Hard to believe they were on the end of day four. If they'd had fresh horses at Maggards . . . oh well, the snow and all. Glanding better be damned glad they got this far. They approached the community with a dusty fan tail behind them, the road already dry. The small vestiges of snow remained only in the deepest shade.

"Where's Thorpe's?" Slocum asked a man on horseback.

"About a quarter on the left. Can't miss it. He's got a wagon yard."

65

"Thanks." And he clucked to the team.

Under the sign, "Thorpe's," he reined the horses to a halt.

"You must be the long lost mail," said a potbellied man, who came out on the porch holding on to his galluses.

"We are, and we need fresh horses."

"Got them. How the hell you ever come over the rim? They said that road was drifted shut. Couple guys went up there and turned around and came back."

"Me and Chris here would have liked to've had wings in places getting here. Where's some food?"

"My old lady's got some inside here. You ain't going on tonight are you?" Thorpe frowned in disbelief at them.

"Yes, soon as we get some food in our bellies."

"That damn mountain ain't—"

"Moon'll be up," Slocum said, considering the clouds were gone. "Yeah, we're going. Oh, where's the outhouse?"

"In back, you can't miss it."

"Good," Slocum said, and motioned for Chris to go ahead. "Get them fresh horse hitched," he said to the man over his shoulder as the two of them headed for the facilities.

"You're a slave driver," she said with a disapproving shake of her head before jerking open the door to the outhouse.

"I promise you a hotel room and hot bath in Preskitt," Slocum said.

She stuck her head out and looked with a frown at him as he undid his pants to pee beside the structure.

"You serious?" she asked with a gesture of disbelief in her look.

"I keep my promises."

"Go ahead," she said to him and grinned. "I've seen it before."

He shook his head at the slap of the door. Whimsically, he thought about her fine slender body under his blankets in midday. About through peeing, he heard the approach of footsteps and quickly finished.

"Get your hands up!"

A cold chill ran up Slocum's spine. The sound of a gun being cocked behind him forced him to raise his hands before he could even button his fly. Damn, who was back there? The voice didn't sound familiar.

"Where is she?"

"Who?" he asked loud enough, he hoped, so that she heard him and stayed put.

"That little bitch."

"I'm sorry, I don't know who you're talking about." Hands held up, he slowly turned around and in the dim light recognized Gill Doyle. "Listen, Slocum, where did you leave her?"

"Her? I left that boy in Fort Wingate."

"She ain't no boy."

"I'll be go to hell. Where's all your backup at, Doyle?" Slocum flexed his fingers.

"They're over at the saloon. I was on my way to join them when I spotted you back here. I figured she run off with you." He shook his head, outlined by the yellow light from the windows in the back of Thorpe's building.

"Can I put my hands down now?"

"I guess. Don't try nothing," Doyle said with a flick of his gun barrel at Slocum. "Murphy told me that was the wildest pussy he ever climbed on. Guess we both missed getting some of it."

"Not this," Slocum said, and drove his fist in Doyle's face.

The impact of Slocum's knuckles to Doyle's jaw snapped the man's teeth together like a spring trap. It sent him backwards, and Slocum's left hand snatched the Colt away from him. Bleary-eyed, lying on his back, Doyle struggled to get up. The outhouse door popped open. Barely in time, Slocum managed to capture the furious Christine, who charged out of the outhouse to do battle with Doyle.

Slocum held her arm in a partial restraint as she kicked Doyle twice in the leg. The shocked man crawfished on his butt across the ground to escape her wrath.

"You no good—" she said through gritted teeth.

"Easy," Slocum said, and swung her around until he felt her fury in his hold begin to ease.

"Doyle," he said. "You try anything again with the two of us—you best have a pine box bought."

"If he won't shoot you, I will," she added, still furious as Slocum herded her toward the front.

"What about my gun?" Doyle called after them.

"You lost it," Slocum said and stuck it in his waistband. Then with his arm encircling her, he directed Chris toward the main building.

"We ain't got time for him," he said to her under his breath to control her anger.

"I ever see that Murphy—"

"I pity him."

"You'll think you pity him."

Slocum wet his cracked lips. Her temper was sure afire and he kind of enjoyed it. Why, she hardly needed any help from him. Doyle was lucky, instead of giving him just a sore jaw, she might of shot him below the belt. Slocum looked back, but in the falling light he saw not a sign of the man. They went inside the lighted room.

A buxom woman with frizzy red hair waved them over to a rough wooden table set with a bowl of frijoles, light bread, and fire-cooked meat on a platter. Slocum guessed it to be deer. The best part of the meal was the homemade butter.

"You must have a cow," he said to the woman as she refilled their coffee cups with a rich, fresh-made brew.

"Sure do. Damn Injuns have stole her twice, but we got her back each time." She straightened and shoved her amble bustline forward. "Them sons a bitches steal her again, I aim to shoot them."

"Guess Injuns need butter too," Slocum said and slathered more on the other half of his biscuit.

"Hmm," the woman snorted and stalked off. "They're too damn lazy to milk her," she said, from the doorway to the kitchen.

"Maybe they don't know how."

Chris was quietly laughing between bites. "Slocum, do you like to see women get mad?" she asked under her breath.

"Naw," he said and went back to eating after a quick check of the front doorway. No sign of Doyle, but he knew they weren't through with him.

Thorpe came inside and hung his soiled canvas coat on a hook. Then, threading his suspenders in the webs of his hands, he strode over and sat down across from Slocum.

"What's been happening? You're the first mail driver we've seen in six weeks."

Slocum explained the past problems and the man nodded. He concluded with, "This run is a tough contract. There's a man we ran into out back named Doyle."

"Yeah, him and two others came in ahead of the snowstorm. What's he after?"

"Trouble. Chris had a run-in with him back at Wingate. I can't understand why he was so hard-pressed to get out here ahead of us." For a long moment, Slocum considered the notion about Doyle and studied the dust-coated deer antlers over the kitchen door. This Doyle business wasn't all over for her. Him and his pards were either running from the law to travel that hard, or else they had other plans.

"He asked a lot of questions about Glanding's deal with me about stabling his horses," Thorpe said and combed his too-long hair back with his fingers.

"He's checked out every stop that Glanding set up," Slocum said, turning the information over in his mind.

Chris looked up from eating and nodded slowlike. "You think he wants the mail contract?"

"I think it must be profitable," Slocum said. "Are Doyle's bunch's saddle horses stabled here?"

Thorpe nodded.

"Make sure we get a good head start to Preskitt, before you let him have them."

"No problem, but going up that canyon out of here, it maybe icy and it ain't much of a road in the daylight." He shook his head in disapproval.

"Any grizzlies up there?" Chris asked, not looking up from her meal.

"Naw," Thorpe said.

"Then he ain't worried," she said and grinned big as she chewed on her mouthful of beans.

"It's damn sure a bear of a mountain," Thorpe said.

"You stall Doyle long enough. We'll worry about the grade. Those horses you hitched shod?"

"They're as good a team as you drove in here."

"Fine. We need to be in Preskitt, sleep a few hours, and head back. We should be back here tomorrow. Feed them blacks good."

"Damn, glad I don't work for you," Thorpe said, acting taken aback by Slocum's expectations. "Kid, you have my sympathy."

Her spoon poised, Chris nodded as if she knew it. "I need that too."

In ten minutes, both of them were outside on the wagon seat. Thorpe promised them again to stall Doyle. Slocum thanked him and set the fresh horses off. He could have sworn someone rushed out of a saloon door in the twilight when they passed it and shouted, "There they go now!" But with the churn of the horses' hooves and the wagon wheels' rush, he wasn't certain.

They crossed the shallow Verde and started the long climb to the top of the snow-covered rim that loomed in the starry night over them. Like a great wall, he thought. He knew the way to the top would be slow, and in places the footing treacherous, but once up there on top, he planned to race for Preskitt.

Chris looked over her shoulder and turned back. "They coming?"

"I suspect that they are." He flicked the reins at the hard-loping team. They could walk when they got to the steep parts.

"What made you think they were checking on the mail run?"

"Funny to me how they tested each place ahead of us. If we don't get this mail through, perhaps after all these delays the government would take the contract away from Glanding."

"He's had lots of bad luck."

"Might not be all bad luck. That renegade Dog Shit might be paid to see that no mail rigs get through." Slocum drew the hard-charging ponies down to a trot. The steepness of the road grade had begun. The ground still only damp, he knew the higher up the mountain they went there would be plenty of ice and snow to cross.

"I told you it was stupid for an Indian to rob a mail wagon. Especially if he couldn't read."

"But not if he was being paid something. I figure he might work cheap too."

"What's Doyle's deal? You figured it out yet?" she asked.

"He ain't enough of a businessman to figure out how to get the mail contract. Secondly, he's new to Fort Wingate. He came with your outfit down from Dodge City to Sante Fe, right?"

"So?"

"I think whoever is behind trying to take the contract from Glanding might have hired Doyle and his men to check it out." He spoke softly to settle the hard-breathing team, who were fighting the reins to charge faster. "Easy, easy, you'll have enough running before this night is over," he promised the anxious horses.

"Slocum, you have no roots. Why?" Chris asked.

He glanced back, saw nothing in the inky starlight, then faced the front. "There's a wanted poster from Fort Scott, Kansas that has a poor resemblance of me on it. A rich man keeps two Kansas deputies on my trail all the time."

"What for?"

"It says murder."

"Was it?"

He shook his head.

"Then why don't you go back and clear yourself."

"Been too long ago now, witnesses are gone. He owns the sheriff, and the judge, and he believes I killed his son. How will that end?"

"So you're on the run?"

"Exactly."

"But you could drive this mail wagon—"

"Until they get word that I'm here and come looking for me."

"Whew. If we don't have time for a bath in Preskitt—" She shrugged her shoulders under the poncho. "I'd forgive you."

"I promised you a bath. You're going to get one."

She hugged his arm. "Damn, I kinda hoped that you needed someone."

"I do," he said, bracing his feet and sawing down the anxious team to a walk. "Just don't know how long I can stay."

"I understand," she said softly and peered at the white stuff. "We're back in the snow."

"I figure we will be all the way up this steep road. It isn't real cold and it may be wet, which could be worse than frozen. I'm walking them from here on."

"Won't Doyle catch us?"

"If he's coming he might. But he better have that pine box paid for if he wants trouble."

She nodded. Slocum threw his head back and raised his gaze to the top lip of the shadowy mountain. They had a long ways to go before they reached the pass above them. Doyle's chance to stop them was on his side.

The two grew silent with the narrowing of the road. The deeper the snow-packed road went into the canyon, the darker the way grew. The uphill pitch increased with each hundred yards. Snaking the wagon around the shiny wet face of the mountain, the team's iron shoes rang and echoed back across the vast gap that fell away from them. So far the animals' hooves were cutting down to the surface, and finding footing. They huffed great clouds of steam with their hard breath. Still straining at the bits, they churned their way up the steep grade, rounding corners, and avoiding the crest.

"Isn't any time to look down," she said and gripped the back of the seat behind his back.

"You won't hurt until you hit way down there," he teased, with the lines tight in his fists. His back muscles braced. Legs hard-pressed in his boots jammed to the dash. It was no place to let up. The horses were still fresh and ready to surge. If he gave them an inch they would lurch forward despite the hard pull.

"Slocum," she said, touching his right arm. "I hear horses coming up the road behind us."

He strained to listen, but above their own sounds, he heard nothing.

"Can you reach under the seat?" he asked.

"I think so. You want a blasting stick?"

"Yes."

"What if it ain't him, Doyle, I mean?"

"We'll set the first one off far enough ahead of them, it will only be a warning."

"What if it don't stop them?"

"We'll know, won't we?"

"Yes," she said, using his knee to steady herself getting down. The rig bucked over some rocks, but she managed to stay in place and soon emerged with two sticks.

"How long should I make the fuse?"

"Leave it long. I don't want these horses spooked too bad by the explosion. The matches are in my shirt pocket."

She dug some out and sat back on the seat. Her hands shaking, she struck one alive in a blinding flare, and soon the fuse sputtered.

"Toss it in the road behind us," he said and stood up, fighting the bits. He knew it would only be minutes before the percussion from the blast would jar the entire canyon.

They rounded a sharp bend, and he glanced back, but couldn't see the bright-burning fuse. Another fifty feet, then a hundred more. The booming report of the blasting stick shook the air. Both horses jumped forward in their collars, but well-braced, he coaxed and sawed them down to a walk.

Then a glop of wet snow struck his head, so wet and

heavy it turned the brim on his hat down, and about blinded him. Cold mush slopped on his shoulders.

"The whole mountain's coming down!" Chris screamed. "It's an avalanche!"

He gave the bits to the team. Great clumps of snow spilled from the mountain face and tumbled on them. The horses charged through the mass. Slocum looked up, but all he could see was more white falling. He urged the animals to go faster.

"Slocum!" she shouted, then another heavy load dropped on them. "We'll be buried alive!"

9

On top of the pass at last, the horses danced impatiently in the silver night. Breathing hard, Slocum and Chris made great vapor clouds. They scooped away the wet snow from the buckboard's canvas cover with their hands. Facing each other, they unloaded all the white stuff that they could and nodded to each other.

"Where do you reckon Doyle is?" she asked.

"He may be digging himself out."

"I hope so. How far is Preskitt?"

"Thirty miles. These horses look all right. I aim to push them." He climbed up, undid the reins, and sat down on the seat. "You ready?"

"Let's go."

Slocum drove the horses at a hard pace up the valley under the starlight. In two-and-a-half hours they topped the last hill, and he reined them down to a trot. Lathered and still ready to go, the animals showed signs of wear, their breathing grew ragged. Before them spilled the yellow lights of Prescott. He had to cut a day off the schedule; he needed to be there in three-and-a-half to even make the turnaround.

He hauled them to a halt before Pasquel's Livery. A

boy and a sleepy-eyed man came out and blinked in dis-belief at them.

"You've got the mail?" the man asked.

"Yes."

"Hallelujah. Benny, you go over and tell them on Whis-key Row, the mail's done finally got here."

"Hey, hold on there. I can't give it out." Slocum frowned at the pair.

"He'll bring the postmaster back too," the man said. "You've run these horses a fur piece."

"They need to be cooled out."

"Benny will do that when he gets back. My name's Tater Biggs."

"Slocum, and that's Chris. Hey, Biggs, we want a bath and a hotel room. Need a fresh team hooked up and the mail going back needs to be loaded and ready in four hours. We leave then."

"I can handle it. Go right over there to the Senator Hotel. They'll fix you up. Your horses and the mail will be ready. There's lots of folks here in Preskitt would buy you a drink for finally getting through with this dang mail."

"I'd like that, but I need to get back to Fort Wingate and I'm over a day behind." Slocum motioned for Chris to head for the hotel across the street.

He caught up with her in a few steps as the first charge of celebrators came out of the nearest saloon of a long row that stood facing the square on the west side. This getting the mail there must be a big deal. They were sure shouting and yelling about it.

"One room?" the desk clerk asked them in the lobby.

"And a hot bath for both of us."

"In the room, it is extra."

"I can pay for the extra," Slocum said. "Get the water up there, we only have a short time to sleep."

"Oh." The clerk tried to see past them. "What is all the commotion out there, anyway?"

"The mail buckboard just got here from Fort Wingate," Slocum said, signing in the guest register.

"Oh, I must—"

"No, you must get that water boiling." Slocum's arm shot over and caught the man by the sleeve. "There will be time for your mail later. If you ever want to get any more mail, we need a bath and some sleep."

"Oh, you two brought it in?"

"Yes. Now go get the water boiling."

"I will. Here is the key, down at the end of the hall on the right."

"How soon is the water coming?"

"In a minute, we have a water heater built into the furnace. We're very modern here in Preskitt. And now that you have delivered the mail, many of us will have Christmas."

"Fine, you have some extra pails?"

"I guess so."

"We'll go with you and help haul the water." Slocum shared a nod with Chris.

"Oh, splendid, sir." The clerk looked anxiously out the front window of the lobby. "I can hardly wait for my letters."

"Just long enough for our bath."

"Oh, yes, this way."

After three trips to the basement, the copper tub in their room was filled and extra of pails of steaming water set by to rinse with. Slocum closed the door on the clerk, turned and nodded to Chris.

"I promised you a bath."

She wrinkled her nose at him and began to undress in the flickering candlelight. She unbuttoned the shirt and her small pear-shaped breasts were soon exposed. She stripped the garment off and he studied the turn of her slender shoulders. Deliberately, she toed off her boots and then shed the pants and underwear. Her long, stemlike leg pointed at the tub, and she tested the water.

"Whew, it will be a hot bath," she said and smiled at him with a hint of a blush on her face. "Slocum, you do deliver what you promise."

Then she eased herself down into the water. Her eyelids

closed as she savored the water's hot embrace. Then she held out her arms for him.

"Come kiss me," she requested.

"Wait till I shave," he said, setting his gear out on the dresser. He pushed off his galluses then deciding that she wouldn't be happy until he kissed her, he went across the room to her.

He bent over, and she locked her arms around him, her mouth bent on smothering him. When he tried to raise up she came with him. Water soon soaked through his shirt, but her hungry mouth fed on his. His hands touched the warm, wet skin on her back. There was no end to her need, until at last they separated.

"That's for the hot water," she said, and busied herself soaping a rag.

"What else you owe me for?" he said at the mirror, soaping his face with a brush.

"Oh, getting me here, beating up Doyle, making love to me on a bedroll. . . ."

He nodded to her while he concentrated on his single edge gliding over his face. The sharp blade came across the skin, shearing off the stubble until he paused to rinse the residue off in the pan of water, and then went back for more.

"Wish we had more time here," he said, looking over at her as she stepped out. The orange lamplight danced on her ivory skin. Whew—for a slender "boy," she made a helluva woman.

His shaving complete, he began to undress. She had drawn a blanket over her against the chill in the room and was wrapped inside it. Seated on the edge of the bed, she kicked her shapely bare legs at him.

'When we get back to Fort Wingate . . ." she trailed off like she wondered but didn't want to ask out loud.

"I plan to turn around and make another trip."

"But what if they find you? Those men you spoke about?"

"Then I'd have to leave," he said, stepping into the tub. The warm water soaked into his legs, then his butt, as he lowered himself into the water. It felt completely relaxing.

"Will they come right away?"

"I doubt it. They were in Texas last I heard of them."

"Looking for you down there?"

"Yes, that's all the Abbott brothers do is track me."

"Heavens," she said, and then made a pained face at him.

"What's wrong?" he asked, pausing with the soap in his hand.

"I want you to hurry."

"Oh," he said, cocking his head to the side and raising an eyebrow at her.

"Damnit Slocum! We don't have all night." She gave him a peeved frown.

"Yes ma'am," he said and bolted up with water sheeting off him. He took the towel and quickly dried as she tore back the bed covers to the sheets.

"Besides, it's cold in here after that hot bath."

"It won't be for long," he said, as he finished drying his sole, hopping around on one foot.

He was in the bed under the covers in an instant. Her smooth skin felt cold. She shivered under his touch as their faces met in a demanding kiss. His hand cupped her small breast, then the pad of his thumb began to rub the rock-hard nipple.

Chris started to moan. Her body began to twist and it pressed to him. Then his finger explored the silky skin between her legs. Her flat belly rose to meet his palm, and when he inserted his finger inside her she cried out.

In moments, with a creak of the bed ropes beneath them, he was on top and her small hand was directing his rigid rod into her. His aching butt drove him forward, guaging deeper and deeper. She threw her head back and cried out in pleasure.

Their pubic bones ground together. Her heels dug into the back of his knees as she forced her belly muscles hard against the ribbed muscles of his stomach. Force against force, they sought the most that pleasure could bring.

Twice she slipped off into release and then recovered, until the bed's protesting ropes grew sharper, and he drove his last ounce of dick into her depths and exploded.

They fell into a faint that mingled with sleep. When he awoke she was curled with her back to him in a fetal position. His hand cradled her stomach.

Startled awake, he could see the pink blush of dawn. He jumped out of bed. They had overslept.

"Chris, we've got to go!"

"Oh God, Slocum, you're such a slave driver," she said, half asleep and, with her hands outstretched, searched for her clothing.

"We're going to beat our own time going back."

"What about Doyle?"

"That snow treatment wasn't enough for him, we've got more."

She warily pulled on her pants. Then she straightened and gave him a good look at her breasts. "What if—-"

"He won't stop us," he said and pulling on his boots, grinned at her. Though he wished he had all day to play with them and her, his mind was on the canyon road. Would it be clear enough to get through? The temperature wasn't that cold. They would have to see what it was like when they got there. More good things about this job. He damn sure hadn't charged Glanding enough.

"I'm coming, I'm coming," she said, hopping around on one foot, pulling her boots on. "Wait for me."

"I will," he said from the doorway. The new day and the trip back to Fort Wingate had begun. They hurried down a quick breakfast of biscuits and eggs.

At the stables, Slocum frowned at the load of mail heaped under the cover on the buckboard. This would never do. He didn't need all that tiring his horses—too damn much loaded on the rig.

"Go get that postmaster. We can't take all that," Slocum said in disgust, and began to undo the tie-downs on the corner of the canvas.

"Everyone was anxious to send their mail—it's been—" Pasquel said.

"The mail will be regular from now on. But that's twice the allotted amount I am supposed to haul."

"No need waking him, I'll help you unload part of it," Pasquel said in defeat.

Chris moved in to help and they soon packed half of the packages and mail sacks into the livery office. Slocum was standing in the doorway and speculated about how far they could go, when a red-faced young man breathing great clouds of vapor and huffing came from across the street.

"Mister! Mister! How did you ever get here?" he gasped.

"Driving a team," Slocum said and went by him.

"I mean I need a story for the newspaper."

"I need to already be in Fort Wingate."

"Do you know what this delivery means to Preskitt and Yavapia County?"

Slocum stepped up on the buckboard, winked at Chris already on the seat, and took his place. "I guess they have mail to read now."

"No, it is far more significant than that."

"Good, I'll see you in a week with more sig-nificant mail." Reins in his hand, he clucked to the ready team. "Get out of here!"

The buckboard left Preskitt and the young reporter standing in the street. The horses charged up the steep hillside street and were Camp Verde bound. A pair of light colored sorrels, they acted full of energy. A sparkling sun warmed the air and only small dots of snow remained under the pines and sage in the open land. When he finally topped the last ridge, he let them race across the valley. Near the top of the pass, he drew them down.

"Wonder how full of snow the road is," he remarked as he let the team catch its breath.

"I wondered that myself. What do you reckon happened to Doyle and them?"

"I hope they were buried alive." He heard the sounds of wagons coming out of the canyon and stood up to see who was coming out. Good, the road down must be open if someone was emerging from there.

Soon the bobbing heads of mules came into sight. He could see there were several teams and obviously multiple wagons behind them. He decided to wait and talk to them.

"They may tell us how it is," he said to Chris, and drove the team toward them.

"Howdy," the gray-bearded outrider said, coming alongside them.

"How's the road?" Slocum asked.

"Clear now, by damn. We shovelled it off to get through. Must've had an avalanche up here. Blessed snow was piled head-high on that road."

"Did it catch anyone?"

"No, but we saw where a horse went off. Killed him, but no sign of the rider, and by damn, we spent two hours clearing all that snow off to get through it."

Slocum thanked him. "Any more wagons coming up?"

"None I know about."

"Good to see you," Slocum said and waved to the drivers of both trains. He passed the two hookups and they went over the rim. Far below the green streaks of winter wheat along the Verde River shown against the pink, reds, and browns of the formations on the north side that stacked up to the lofty far rim.

Chris hugged his arm. "Score one for us getting them to clear the road. Wonder if it got Doyle."

He nodded, sawing on the sorrels to keep them in a walk. The way was steep and slushy. He needed no problems with them. He glanced over the side. Far below and down the steep mountainside, he spotted a saddled dead horse sprawled on top of a large rock formation.

"Look down there," he said with a toss of his head to the side of the great canyon yawning beside them.

"It's a dead horse with a saddle on it. That's the one those freighters saw?"

"Damned if I know. But he's a long ways down there. It would have been a helluva ride."

"I never knew what they rode."

Slocum shook his head, too busy trying to control the team to worry much about Doyle and his thugs. The horses danced and pranced, hooves slapping melting snow and making it even harder to negotiate the sharp curves in the sheer, wet gray wall the road clung to. A ball formed in his stomach; should he tell Chris to get out and walk?

The front hub scraped on the rock face. He adjusted the team and shared a quick nod with her. His heart beat in his throat. Boot soles jammed to the dash, the muscles in the backs of his legs cramped. He leaned back to avoid being pitched over.

The outside horse's hind feet slipped on the wet loose snow and scooted under him. The right horse shied when he lurched around to regain his footing. All Slocum could see was the edge, and nothing for hundreds of yards underneath them. The horse continued to struggle for his footing, but his hooves found little security. Then he went down on his knees and the inside horse reared in panic.

"Chris, get over the back!" he shouted to her. "Get off!"

Somehow his sawing eased the fighting horse back on his haunches. Then his footing went out. Slocum wanted to close his eyes. In a second, if those horses didn't settle down, they, the wagon, and all would be over the edge. The strength drained from his upper torso; he felt his cheeks grow numb. Both of his leg muscles cramped.

At last, the outside horse planted four feet, and they held. Slocum fought the frightened other horse to a standstill. A long, quiet moment passed. Both horses trembled in place under the harness as if they too realized the closeness of the life and death situation. Slocum dared to breathe and swallowed hard again.

"Oh hell," Chris said, in a gasp of relief. "There was a grizzly on this mountain."

Slocum settled back on the seat, the acute tension slowly deflated from his body and mind. "Yeah, and there's only five more miles of this to go."

10

Farther down, the mountain road turned dry with only hints of snow, and the warmer midday temperature of the valley forced them to shed their ponchos. At last off the mountain, he set the team into a charge the last miles to Camp Verde and Thorpe's. The wind was in their faces, Chris hung on to the seat for dear life, and Slocum used the lines and his braced legs to keep himself in. In places, the buckboard soared in the air and threw up a fine fan of dust when he swung it around sideways on the corners.

He reined up for the river and they both dismounted for a long drink belly-down on the bank. Stretching her arms over her head, she finished, and then shook her head.

"I thought we were goners up there."

"He didn't want us today," Slocum said and grinned at her.

"Yeah, good thing," she said and moved under him, his arm on her shoulder. They walked back to the rig. "Wonder if that rider lived."

"Guess we'll know more in Camp Verde." He took her by the narrow waist and boosted her on the rig.

She looked back and shook her head. "You sure are not one to worry much."

"Oh, that back there?" He tossed his head to the tow-

ering range above them. "Now that's over, I'm more concerned how to be back in Wingate in two-and-a-half more
days."

She looked at the sky. Seated beside her, he took the
lines and then smiled. "Be a damn sight easier if we had
wings."

"A whole lot easier."

It was past noon when they pulled up before Thrope's.
Slocum stepped down and she hurried off to use the facilities.

"You ain't far off that schedule of yours," Thorpe said,
coming out on the porch. "Go inside and grab some grub,
we'll have your blacks in harness by then."

Slocum looked around, saw nothing out of place.
"What about Doyle?"

"They got caught in an avalanche last night in the canyon. That young one lost his horse. The old man broke
his arm. Guess they're lucky to be alive. Surprised you
got over it and back."

"Some freighters cleaned it out to get through before
we got there."

"Omaha Fredricks and his bunch. I seen them pull
through here headed that way at daybreak."

"Anyone coming off the Crook Road?" Slocum asked.

"Yeah, had a couple light wagons come over it. They
said lots of it's melted. I've got some bad news. Doyle
and that boy rode that way earlier. They may be laying
for you up there."

Slocum nodded and Chris joined them.

"What's that?" she asked.

"Doyle rode east a little earlier."

"Oh shit," she said, with a cross look of concern written
on her face for him.

"Don't worry, we can handle them." Slocum gathered
her under his arm and directed her inside to eat. It had to
be a quick meal again. Doyle's actions filled his thoughts.
Would he try to stop them? Obviously surveying the trip,
and learning the waystations was all part of Doyle's plan.
Not letting the mail get through must also be.

The food filled a hollow place in his belly. Slocum hurried her to get back on the road. Outside in the sunshine, he thanked Thorpe and his wife, took the lines for the blacks, and climbed on the seat.

"Thanks," Chris said to them with a wave from beside him. The lurch of the horses threw her back on the seat. Slocum waved the lines at them and sent the team into a run. They had a mountain range to cross and he wanted to be on top of it before the sun set. Though he doubted they could make it in such a short while, he planned to push the stout team to try.

Midafternoon, they shrugged on their ponchos at the the pinion juniper elevation. No sign of Doyle, though Slocum felt certain he recognized a fresh set of prints with narrow shoes. If it was either Doyle's or the boy's then he could identify it when he ran across it again.

With a glance to the west and his acknowledging the sinking afternoon sun, they began to get back into patchy snow. First, white clumps only spotted the shade, then the road grew steeper and wetter. Gurgling small rivulets rushed off the mountain face from the melt. Then on top of the grade he reined up to study the steep downhill shelf that clung to the mountain side and disappeared a quarter-mile ahead to round a sheer face. The snow looked packed, and he eased the anxious horses into a strained walk to start them downhill.

"Another tough one," Chris said and pursed her lips together.

"Isn't there a flat at the bottom of this?" Slocum asked.

"Yes. We stopped there."

He smiled at the memory of their first tryst. "Ah, yes. Somehow I have an itch under my collar about that place. Be a perfect place for a holdup." He fought to keep the two animals in check. So far their horseshoes cut through and tossed the pads of it with each turn of their ankles. It was the balled-up snow in their frogs that made them slick-footed like skis. That was what happened above Camp Verde to the other team.

"How will we do it?" she asked.

"Get out a stick of dynamite with the longest fuse. We'll have it lit and ready when we come off the mountain. I figure we can scatter them with it going off, plus fire your Colt at them."

"What if we can't see them?"

"Then we'll call it our own New Year's party."

"How about a Christmas party?"

"Yeah. That isn't far away, is it?"

She gave him a look of uncertainty and slipped off the seat to her hands and knees on the floorboard to find another stick of blasting powder. At last, she drew it out and scrambled back up. Out of breath, she fought to regain her composure.

"Now what?"

He sawed harder on the blacks' mouths. They were wanting to run and with the drop-off on the left side made for buzzards to float over, he wanted them slowed more. The mare began to prance, and Slocum swore at her, "Damnit, quit!"

He wondered how much longer he could hold them back. Chris reached under Slocum's poncho and drew out two matches from his shirt pocket. The red stick clamped between her legs, she sat back.

"When we make this curve, I may let these buggers run. That would shock them too. My biggest hope is to catch them off guard."

"When do I light this?"

"You must be a little less afraid of it going off in your hand than before."

She quickly nodded.

"Then before I give the horses their lead. I'll tell you to light it."

"Fine."

He glanced over. It was not fine, he could tell not only by her voice but by the pale look on her face. But she still had plenty of grit. He hoped this settled Doyle's hash. In his heart, he doubted it would, but perhaps it would make the man realize it would be better to not bother with them again.

The horses were past holding back when he said, "Now!" to her. She struck the match and the wrapped paper fuse began to sparkle. He gave the bits to the black as they rounded the bend, the flat lie before them. The pair hit the collars and came off the mountain in a rumble of wagon wheels. Slocum switched the lines to his left hand and between bumps and bounces he drew his Colt.

There still was plenty of primer cord. She clung to the back of the seat with one white-knuckled hand while her right one carried the red stick like a torch. Slocum saw movement in the brush. The turn of a horse butt was all he could make out. With the Colt, he began blasting away at the thick junipers.

"We go by there, toss it in those bushes," he said to her.

She nodded and the wagon and team swept by the grove of thick boughs that rose overhead high to a man on horseback. Chris drew back her arm and flung it hard. Slocum watched the red stick go flying over the very top of the evergreens and begin an arc downward into them.

"Good throw!" he said.

Then the explosion struck their backs. Holding onto the reins, Slocum glanced back in time to see lots of flying boughs and needles. No sign of Doyle, but he knew they had gotten close.

He settled in the seat and nodded to her. "That should settle their hash."

Pale faced, she agreed in relief. "I thought you were never going to tell me to throw it."

"You did good," he bragged on her, and both of them checked their back trail as the blacks raced on over the flat. No sign of Doyle or his henchmen. Slocum hoped that finished the matter, but an inkling in the back of his mind told him it only put the conflict off for another time and place.

The sun set and caught them fighting the steep grades. Slocum held the blacks down to a hard walk climbing the last vestiges of the mountain rim. He finally rested the horses when they topped out on the starlighted flats. She went off to find a comfort station. He did the same beside the wagon, then he dug out blankets for them to pull on against the rising wind.

When she returned, he held it up and dropped it over her head and shoulders. "That should help ward off some of the damn cold," he said.

"Thanks. We getting any sleep tonight?"

"When we get to Denton's we can sleep a few hours. You going to make it?"

"Sure, just tired, that's all."

He studied the north star. They should be there by midnight. "We'll get there before you know it."

"Oh, there aren't any more loaded blasting sticks down there. That was the last one."

"Thanks, I'll have to fix some more."

She stood up in the buckboard and tried to look to the south as he climbed on. "Maybe we got them?"

"Maybe," he agreed and seated, set the blacks off northward under the wide array of stars. These mail run problems weren't simply renegade Indians and bad weather hurting Glanding's operation, there was an active campaign to stop all the deliveries. Maybe he'd learn the source of trouble before they got back to Fort Wingate.

The sharp night wind caused his eyes to tear as they swept across the rolling sea of sage and grass. The grunts and hard breathing of the blacks carried above the rattle of the wheels. The team acted like they enjoyed the unfettered race. In the lane between the dark outline of sage and grass they sped toward Denton's Ranch.

"That you, Slocum?" the rancher shouted, coming from the house in a barrage of barking dogs.

"Yeah. We made it here."

"What do you need now?" the man asked, holding up the dim lantern to see them.

"A bunk and a few hours shut-eye. I want to be woke up before dawn and headed on our way."

"When did you leave Preskitt?" Denton asked.

"This morning," Chris said, unpacking their bedrolls.

"Go on in there and get some sleep. I'll cool off these horses and I'll have your fresh ones hitched up and ready so you can be on your way before the sun winks."

"Thanks Denton," Slocum said, barely able to keep his eyes open. He followed her inside. Fully dressed, they laid down to sleep on the floor in their bedrolls. The warmth of the crackling fire felt good on Slocum's sleepy face when he closed his tired eyes.

Sometime in the night, he thought he heard the dogs barking. But soon he went back to sleep. It was the coarse, familiar-sounding voice and muzzle of a gun in his face that brought him awake.

"Gawdamn you and your fucking dynamite!" Doyle growled.

"Did we get close?" Slocum asked, being jerked up by his shirt.

"Sorry, they jumped me outside," Denton said in apology. Slocum could see the rancher was bound and tied in a high back chair. They shared a private look of anger and disgust. Slocum shook his head over this new predicament. Damn, they sure caught him unawares.

"Get up you, little bitch!" It was Everett Cone rousing Chris up that made Slocum jerk around to look in that direction.

"You want to die?" Doyle made his point with the spent-smoke smelling muzzle of his gun in Slocum's face. "It's our turn to try some of that pussy."

"I'll be fine," she said, standing on her feet, her words for Slocum's sake. Narrow eyed, she tossed her head in defiance at the younger outlaw.

"Get them clothes off," Cone ordered. "I been waiting for this for a long while." He gave a grab at his crotch as if considering screwing her.

"You! Get over in that chair," Doyle ordered, and Slocum moved slow to obey him, hoping for an opening to wrench the pistol away from him and turn the scene. The time would be short; if he didn't do something soon, Cone would rape her. He saw the intent in his flush face.

"Sit down," Doyle ordered, never taking his eye off him.

Perhaps if she undressed, Doyle might be distracted. The outlaw caught his right wrist in a loop and tightened the rope on it. Slocum had one last chance, but the gun in Doyle's other hand reiterated his threat. Nothing Slocum could do, but let his other wrist be captured and his hands bound behind his back. Soon he sat hog-tied to the chair and was forced to watch her undress for Cone. The younger one was toeing off his boots. His undivided attention was on Chris, who stood bare-breasted before him, acting like he didn't exist. With deliberate fingers, he began to unbuckle her pants.

"You touch her, you're a dead man," Slocum warned, the rage stirring in him so deep, he felt he should be able to rip asunder the ropes.

"Ha, the only dead men in this room is you and him." Doyle laughed over his shoulder, standing with both hands on his hips enjoying the show.

Soon, she stood fully undressed, clutching her arms over her chest. Cone struggled to undress himself. His pants turned inside out, they did not want to come free, and he was forced to sit on his butt atop the bedrolls to untangle them. At last in his underwear, breathing like a runaway horse, he pealed them off and stood buck-naked. His right hand stroked his tool, and he advanced on her.

She never looked up. He forced her onto the bed and followed her down. Then he squirmed on top of her, trying to get it in. His cussing and struggle to stab his half-limp dick inside of her only drew the deepest rage from Slocum.

"Let me do it!" Doyle said and dropped his pants. Obviously his erection was working, and he pulled the grumbling Cone aside, and on his knees waded across the bed to where she lay.

"I'll show you a real dick," Doyle promised her as he spread her white legs apart in the yellow lamplight.

She gave a short cry of distress at his entry, then became silent; Doyle's labored grunting began. His hairy butt bobbed up and down only adding to Slocum's rage.

Slocum he strained at the ropes behind his back. Cone's bare hatchet butt turned toward Slocum as he watched his boss rape her. Slocum wanted to kick the outlaw hard enought to implant a boot one-foot up his ass. The rope around his left hand gave a little. The gurgled sounds in Doyle's throat as he began to come inside her only blackened his mind.

"Now you got it hard?" Doyle asked.

Cone pushed Doyle aside. "I'll screw her till she screams."

"Oh, yeah," Doyle said, putting his tool back in his underwear, slipped off the bed and hoisted up his pants to refasten them. His attention was on Cone as he stabbed his dick at her.

Slocum's right hand slipped out of the first loop and he eased the second one free, keeping them both back to not expose his condition. He motioned for Denton to get Doyle's attention behind the man's back.

"You ain't getting away with this!" Denton said aloud and raised up to strain at his binds.

"What? Us screwing her?" Doyle asked with a grin.

Slocum stared at the wooden grips. Could he reach the butt of Doyle's gun? Even though his legs and the rest of his body were still wrapped up in rope—but if he only had hold of Doyle's weapon. The risk for him was to be on the floor under the chair afterwards and still be tied up. He would be helpless—but he might have the Colt in his hand. That would be the powershift in this whole scene. Cone's gun lay atop of a pile on the floor with his clothes. Slocum planned to cover that when he fell forward. The only thing was, if he missed Doyle's gun, he'd seal his own fate. No matter about himself, the grunting sounds of Cone's rutting on top of Chris's body branded in his mind told him what he must do.

Slocum shot his right hand out and used his toes to propel himself forward. His grasp closed on the smooth wooden handle. Then he wrenched the Colt loose, spinning Doyle around, as Slocum, with the revolver in his grasp, sprawled head-first on the cabin floor. Shock-faced at the loss of his gun, Doyle decided in a moment to sprint for the doorway. Slocum hindered by ropes and the chair, rolled over, cocked the hammer, and took aim at Doyle's back. Released in haste, his first wild shot after Doyle drew a cloud of chocking gunsmoke that boiled in the room.

Still pinned under the chair, he heard Cone scream, and the outlaw fell off the bed on top of Slocum and the chair he was still tangled in. Chris dove off the bed at Cone, her blows flying like a windmill.

"He's going for a rifle," Slocum said, wriggling out of the rope and chair. The naked Chris pummelled the screaming boy under her with both her fists. Slocum kicked and twisted to free himself of the rope coils.

At last, he found his way free of his binds. A quick check reassured him, she obviously had the cowering Cone defeated; Slocum rushed to the open doorway. He dropped to the floor on an instinct, realizing the back light in the room would frame him as a target. Seconds later, a rifle slug out of the night sent splinters of wood showering down on him. He returned fire with the Colt at the unseen Doyle.

Then came the thunder of hooves in the night, and Slocum raised up on all fours. The notion came to him in disgust that Doyle had fled. For a long moment, he straightened his stiff back, still on his knees, rubbed his calloused hand over his mouth, and considered what he must do next.

Denton had dragged the naked Cone by the arm to the door. "I say we hang this sumbitch."

Slocum looked at the downcast outlaw. "That's one vote."

"How're you voting?" Denton asked.

"Chris, he wants to know how you're voting?" He could see she was dressing and, by the twitch of her shoulders, crying as well.

He moved over to comfort her, sticking the Colt in his waistband. "I'm sorry, I did all I could."

"I knew they would kill you. How did you eve—" She hugged his waist and buried her face in his chest. "Doyle got away?"

"Yes, he ran. What about Cone?"

"I don't care."

"He don't deserve anything more."

"Since you're all so set on lynching me, let me dress," Cone said.

"Put on your pants," Slocum said. He bent over and tossed them to him, and they let him pull them on.

He and Denton took the outlaw from the house out into the cold night. No sign of Doyle, Slocum decided, peering off into the starlit rolling sagebrush and grassland. The rancher threw a rope over the cross-arm piece. Shirtless, Cone shivered in the cold night air, his hands tied behind his back. Denton fashioned the noose on his neck while Slocum went for his horse.

"You got anything to say?" Denton asked, when Slocum returned with it.

"Yeah, fuck both of you, and her too."

Slocum bit his tongue and they hoisted Cone onto his horse. Denton secured the end of the rope. One slap, the horse bolted away and the outlaw danced on the end of the hemp.

Twenty minutes later with the fresh team harnessed, Slocum climbed on the buckboard in the chill of the gray dawn. The light wind swung the limp body back and forth under the cross-arm. He nodded ready to the withdrawn Chris beside him huddled under the blankets.

"Thanks. See you," he said to Denton, and the man nodded. Slocum had offered to cut Cone down, but Denton said he would handle it and the burial. He slapped the lines to the fresh team and they charged northeastward.

The wagon wheels churned light dust in their wake. Slocum wished he had the right words to comfort her. It would be a long day, but he intended to make the Little Colorado crossing before they slept.

"Doyle's out there, ain't he?" she asked over the wagon's rumbling and the drum of hooves.

"Yes, he's out there."

"What will you do about him?"

"He won't hurt you again. Not ever."

"It's not me I'm worried about," she shouted, holding her hat down with her arm.

"Don't worry about me."

"I will, Slocum." She hugged his arm tight. "I will, until that sumbitch is dead."

11

"No, I ain't seen that worthless turd, Doyle," Kay McNeal said, taking down the corral bars in the cool midmorning sunshine. "Not hide nor hair of him since before you two went through, but I'll damn sure lower my sights on the worthless outfit if he shows up."

"Good," Slocum said and led the sweaty horses into the pen to change harness to the fresh ones.

"You two made good time, considering all that happened to you." She shook her gray head in disbelief. "Why, them two ain't no better than damn dogs. Old Denton and you did the right thing. And I'll sure put Doyle out of his misery if he ever comes around here."

"Be careful, Kay. I think that Doyle's been hired to stop the mail wagon from getting through. He might come back here and try to hurt you."

"He better come with plenty of smoke. Why do you think that?"

"He's been asking too many questions, and I figured it was more over stopping the mail wagon than Chris. Doyle is still dangerous, watch yourself," Slocum said with an armload of harness to throw on the fresh horse. "He could hurt you."

"I'll keep an eye out for him. Whoa!" she said and

jerked on the bridle to make the horse stand still for him.
He slung the leather and chains over the animal's back
and began to separate them out. Kay took the opposite
side, and soon the the straps were in place, and Slocum
went to the other sweat-soaked animal and removed his
set. Kay caught and brought the second big bay in close.
Slocum quickly tossed the harness on him, and in a minute the team was ready to lead out.

Chris came from the house with the bread and meat
Kay sent her after. Slocum finished hitching his side, and
Kay coupled hers. He straightened and smiled at Chris
after he stepped back. They were ready.

"There's some water to wash it down with," Chris said
and put the pail on the wagon before the seat for him to
dipper it. Then she presented him the sandwich, heaped
full of meat.

Holding it in both hands, he took a big bite. The fresh
sourdough bread and smoked meat drew the saliva in his
mouth. He chewed thoughtfully, thinking about the road-
miles left between them and Fort Wingate. A good team
hookup at the trading post, they could push on to the last
stop—maybe they would have fresh horses there this
time. He could hope Pearcy had things organized by the
time they drove up to Maggard's place. The notion of it
niggled him as he chewed and washed his food down with
the sweet water from the bucket.

The two women went off to talk under a gnarled cot-
tonwood while he ate. Perhaps Kay could say something
that would comfort Chris. Over the night he had tried to
think of ways he might. The attack left her numb and
withdrawn, despite his best effort to help her. Damn that
Doyle.

At last he finshed, wiped his hands on the front of his
pants, took a last deep drink, put the dipper in the wooden
bucket, and climbed onto the seat. He drove the anxious
team to the trees and handed Kay the pail.

"Ready, Chris?"

"Yes." She hurried around and joined him on the seat.

"You two make a damn tough team. Old Glanding better be glad he's got you. Beats the hell out of me how he'll find anyone else to do it." Kay shook her head and then looked at Chris. "Take care girl, that Doyle will get his sooner or later. If not on earth, maybe the old devil will run a hot poker up his butt."

Slocum laughed aloud at her effort to demonstrate how to do it. Chris even chuckled at her directions and he swung the team sharply around.

"Thanks, and see you, Kay," he said and they left her place at a dead run. The sun was past the zenith and he wanted to be at the Little Colorado Crossing before it set. The rolling country east of there wouldn't be bad by starlight to Maggards.

Chris turned back and looked. "She's got a real heart of gold."

"And sounds like a lion with her old gravel voice."

Chris nodded at his words as if more content. That made him feel better, and he pressed the fresh ponies onward in a drum of hooves, swirling dust and the cold wind that swept their faces. It would be a long ways to the crossing. He twisted to check their back trail, and then turned back again. Nothing to see, but Kay's small ranch fading from sight in the twisted cloud of dirt.

They raced with few words. Both under their blanket ponchos they rocked on the seat, as the wagon dropped off long grades and hurried up the other side, while the sun offered little heat. Slocum's shoulders grew stiff fighting the bits. Miles rolled by, until at last satisfied it was time to rest the team, he sawed them down on a mesa and drew them to a halt.

Chris went off on the right side; she stood beside the wagon and emptied her bladder in the dust. Finished at last, he watched a hawk circle in the sky.

"We making that schedule?" she asked, as he felt the wagon move under his butt.

"Yeah," he said and turned as she came around.

"How will he try to to stop us?"

He reached out and drew her against his chest. She fit

in place in his arms for the first time since several tries after Denton's.

She buried her face in his blanket and hugged him hard. He drew her face up and looked at her.

"Damn Slocum, it wasn't your fault. They didn't get a virgin."

"I guess I feel I shouldn't let you come back with me knowing them bastards would be somewhere between Preskitt and New Mexico."

"Why? Cause I was a girl instead of a boy? Hell, I wasn't the first girl ever raped."

"I still blame myself for anything you went through because of me," he said, not looking at her, and rocking her side to side.

"You weren't there when my stepfather crawled in my bed with a dong big as a horse's dick either."

"No, but I'd have sent him to his reward, had I known about it."

"I know where he is. He's down on the St. Louis docks panhandling drinks and sleeping under sacks."

"You know that?"

"Yeah. Couple of years ago, Vince found ole Woolson for me." She nodded. "Vince offered to feed him to the catfish, but I told him no. The way he was living I figured was worse for that old boar than getting him out of this world."

"Your maw know what he did to you?"

"He beat her with stove wood. What could she do?"

"You were how old?"

"Twelve. My real father got killed in a timber accident. A tree they were cutting down bounced back off the stump and struck him in the chest. Crushed him. He never breathed twice. Woolson was a widower and neighbor who lived down the way. She had no choice but to marry him, or the four of us would have starved."

"These men that killed Vince?" he asked.

"They must have been wanted, or some he'd arrested before and wanted revenge."

"No names?"

She shook her head, then pushed the hat off her head and with her fingers combed her short blond hair back. Then she closed her eyes and hugged him.

"Bastards," she raged.

"Amen. Let's go girl," he said and took her by the waist and tossed her up on the buckboard. His action drew a smile and she poised her lips and kissed him as he climbed on the seat. He drew a deep breath, unwrapped the reins, then turned back to her, and she kissed him again.

Her hand slid down his cheek and she looked at him hard. "Slocum, I may be bad luck for you."

"Luck's what you make it, and we're changing ours," he said and sent the team racing off along the watercourse lined with dusty brown willows.

She hugged his right arm and the miles rolled under the iron rims.

With the setting sun over their shoulders, they drove into Markam's trading post, and several sleepy-eyed Navajos looked up as the buckboard made an arc of fine dust.

"Señor Slocum?" Pasquel shouted from the porch and hurried to greet them.

"We need a quick meal and fresh horses, *mi amigo*."

"It will be. Go tell Juanita, she will have the food ready pronto. I will have the boys hitch up the fresh horses. You are running hard, no?" Pasquel took the reins to drive the horses around back of the post to change teams.

Slocum followed Chris up the steps into the adobe-rock building. The smell of wool, tobacco, and spices filled the air. Slocum found Juanita and waved off her offer of a room, saying they only needed food and must be on their way.

The brown-faced woman hurried off to arrange it.

Chris wet her lips and grinned. "Be kinda nice to sleep on a real bed."

"I promise you—"

"I know," she said. "A hot bath and a clean hotel room when we get there. By damn, I'm holding you to it too."

They took seats at the empty table. When they came inside, Slocum looked over the crowd in the place and decided nothing was out of the ordinary. He closed his wind-burned eyes and clasped his hands on the tabletop. This was a lot tougher run than he even thought it would be.

"These men looking for you?" She reached over and closed her fingers over his.

"The Abbott brothers."

"Yes. How will I know them?"

"You ever seen an Appaloosa horse?"

She shook her head.

"Lyle rides a big black horse with a white blanket that has small black moons in it. You can't miss the damn thing. Ferd's the younger one. Both have bushy beards."

"They ever catch you?"

"Once or twice, but I managed to get away."

"What are they?"

"Two Kansas deputies. A rich man pays their expenses."

"You told me that." She shook her head, bewildered. Two young girls brought their heaping plates of food. Frijoles, brown meat, peppers, and corn with plenty of white tortillas on another plate, still hot to the touch. He took one and began to spoon on the contents of his plate.

"I simply have to keep an eye out for them. They get word from someone where I'm at and they come riding. So I'm forced to move on. Sometimes without even a good-bye."

She pointed the white tortilla in her hand at him. "You better not run out on me. I want to go with you."

"Chris," he said, taking a moment to chew his bite. "There may not be time."

"Oh, men," she said, and with impatience looked at the exposed rafters. Then she went back to eating. A fact, not missed by Slocum. Good, she might recover from the whole thing.

"I know," she said and reached over to capture his hand

on the tortillas. "A hot bath and fine room for the two of us in Fort Wingate."

He nodded, she let go, and he went on making another. Whew, they had a long night ahead.

He sure wanted to be in Fort Wingate by noon of the next day. Horses better be ready at Maggard's. Why did he worry so? No telling about Pearcy and his dog stew. He bet Chris wouldn't eat a thing there even if she was famished. He took a good swallow of the red wine and closed his eyes. They weren't back to Fort Wingate yet. Their biggest challenge might still lie ahead.

"Señor, they're ready when you are." Pasquel stood above them.

"*Muchas gracias.* This Navajo renegade, Dog?" Slocum asked.

"Ah, they say he is out there. Someone sold him new guns and ammunition."

"Maybe they gave it to him?"

"Huh? Who would do that?"

"Someone who doesn't want the mail to get through, so they can take over the contract."

"That would be bad business."

"There are people like that."

"How else could he get new rifles and ammunition?" Pasquel shook his head in disbelief over the fact. "I think you are right. Be careful señor, and you too," he motioned to Chris.

"She will," Slocum said and heard the man whistle through his teeth.

"You have many surprises, Señor Slocum."

"We may need some more to get back to Wingate."

"*Via con dios.*"

Slocum thanked him, and they hurried outside. The sun set behind a purple streak. He unwrapped the reins, and she put her hand on his arm.

"I hope this food holds me, because I'm not eating with that damn Pearcy."

"Don't blame you." He flicked the lines at the fresh horses and left in a bolt. It would be a long drive through the night to Maggard's.

12

"Something's wrong here, Slocum!" Chris screamed from beside him on the seat. In the starlight, she struggled to free the shotgun from the scabbard in the dash. Slocum wheeled the horses around in a sharp u-turn that threatened to upset the buckboard in an acrid cloud of smoke from the burned-out buildings that faced them. Another disaster at Maggard's was all he could think, laying the lines to urge on the team. The final change station had been destroyed. With forty miles left to Fort Wingate and the inky night lit only by stars, they had a long ways to go.

She twisted right and left, swinging the scattergun around and searching for any sign of an attacker. They reached the main road, and Slocum braced his feet, swinging the horses to the left and eastward. Only good thing was that so far, they had not drawn any obvious pursuit.

"I wonder what happened back there," Slocum said, hauling the horses down to a trot to save them for the distance.

"They did a good job of it. Looked like they even burned down the corrals. Wonder what they did to Pearcy," she mused, with another check of their back trail.

"He may not be amongst the living."

"Didn't he say that Maggard beat up that renegade once?"

"Yes, he did."

"Well, with plenty of ammunition, they might have come back to even the score."

Slocum agreed. It also might be a part of the scheme to destroy the chances of Glanding holding on to the mail contract. There had to be someone behind that effort smarter than Doyle. A money person, because Doyle didn't have his last pay. The whole thing only grew worse and there was nothing he could do about it out there, driving the weary horses that should have been switched. They'd have made Wingate by midnight with fresh horses, but with the present ones, which had been pushed since Markam's, it would be sunup before getting back. If their luck held.

A cold wind out of the north swept the tabletop country and seared his face. Slocum wondered if winter would ever release its hold. Not for months: they still had January, February, and March before the April winds drove out the chill. The lines grasped tight in his cold hands, he urged the team to keep up their trot each time they slacked off.

Chris finally put up the greener. A jingle of the chains and creak of the harness joined the drum beat of the horses' hooves and the ring of the iron rims. Slocum glanced over and nodded his approval at her. They made a tough-enough team. In a few more hours they would be the first to deliver the roundtrip Preskitt mail. Not bad, considering all they'd been through.

"You promising me a bath and a bed in Wingate?" she asked, hugging his arm.

"Yes, ma'am. That and more," he said with a wide grin.

"Oh?" Then she put her head on his shoulder for a minute. "Can this trip be made in a week?"

"Yeah, if it don't snow like a chicken picking, we can do it."

"Guess we can do about anything?"

"About," he agreed, reining the team up for a brief rest. "Ten minutes."

"No time to build a fire?" she teased and bounded off the seat on her side.

"Sure be nice," he said, rubbing his hands together to warm them. She didn't go far in the night. He looked around for any sign of pursuit. Not likely, Indians hated the darkness and the fact probably saved their hides back at Maggard's. She came around the wagon and hugged him.

"Wasn't so cold—"

"You'd what?" he asked, amused at her.

"I'd get out the bedroll."

"A real shame, but we can wait."

"I guess we'll make another run back to Preskitt?"

"I planned to."

"You better not leave me out of those plans."

"I won't," he said and rocked her back and forth against him. They had too many clothes on to appreciate the belly-rubbing, and still the chill of the air sought him. Damn, it was simply plain cold.

On their way again, they dropped into the canyon country with giant rock walls looming over them. The horses tired, and making them trot all the time became more of an effort. He let them walk up the steeper grades. His eyes focused ahead into the distance, he wondered how much longer until dawn spread over the horizon. Wouldn't be long.

They came off the final grade and the few lights of Fort Wingate twinkled in the distance. Weary and wind-whipped, he found some new strength and flicked the lines at the horses to hurry in the final surge. They too seemed to realize their barn was ahead, for they took on new strength and charged into the collars.

Slocum stood against the dash to rein them up before the stageline's dark offices and drove them into the side yard. He tied off the reins, jumped down, and climbed the back steps. His fist pounded on the door. At last a light came on.

"That you Slocum?" a sleepy, hoarse voice called out.

"It ain't your uncle Bob," he said, glancing around to where she stood behind him.

"Where in the hell have you been?" Glanding asked, opening the door for them, and sweeping his hair forward. His shirttail out, the man looked disheveled.

"We've been dodging renegades and hired outlaws."

"Hired what?"

"You have lots of enemies. I think they have been the reason that you haven't gotten any mail through."

Glanding dropped to a chair as if too weak to stand any longer. "Enemies. Who?"

"Who wants the mail contract?"

"Bruce Seaman. But he—"

"He wouldn't hire some thugs to stop us and learn all about your stations." Slocum shook his head. Whether the man believed him or not, someone wanted his mail run stopped. Damn, what did it take? "Who else bid on it."

"Mason, Martin, and . . . some guy lives in Sante Fe." Glanding acted like he wasn't certain of the name.

"You have got some big-time opposition, whoever they are."

Glanding shrugged his thick shoulders. "I can imagine— who did you say they hired?"

"Gill Doyle and two others. Two of them aren't around any more, and Doyle, by this time, has more hired hands, if my guess is right."

"What happened to the two others?"

"One had a horse wreck and the other hung himself."

"Oh."

"No, oh, they burned down Maggard's ranch yesterday, before we could get there and change our horses."

"Burned Maggard's?"

"Yes, we suspect the renegade Navajos under Dog Shit did that, but we didn't have time to check that out."

"I'm going to the fort and talk to the Major."

"You can talk to whoever you want. You need someone much more dependable than Maggard anyway. His man turned your horses out and fed your grain to his hog."

"You serious?"

"As serious as can be," Chris added.

"Slocum, I'm sorry. I underestimated this thing. I thought some renegades were all that was robbing them wagons. But you think someone is out to stop me?"

"I don't know who from Adam's off ox, but someone wants you to fail at this and did a damn good job of trying to stop us. Come on, Chris, we're going to get a bath and some sleep."

"When can you go back? I've got all kinds of Christmas mail."

"You got two buckboards?" Slocum asked.

"I can get them ready." Glanding's eyes searched the two of them.

"You have at least two good teams at each stop, but Maggard's," Slocum said, going over the notion of each of them driving a rig.

"I can handle that. I'll send two teams out there today and have my men meet you near the territorial line."

"Don't just send some poor boys. Arm them and make certain they're tough enough, that's where Dog Shit and his boys hang out."

"When can you leave?"

"Twenty-four hours."

Glanding looked a little disappointed, then he nodded toward Chris. "He going to drive the other team?"

"Yes, she will."

"She?"

"It's too dang complicated to explain. Don't you say a word either. You have it all ready, we'll make the run with both rigs."

"She costs the same?" Glanding asked pained.

"Of course. Come on, we've got bathing, eating, and sleeping to do," Slocum said to her and put his hand on her shoulder to guide her toward the door.

13

The round tub sat in the middle of the bathhouse floor, with Chris's shapely white legs draped over the side of it. Slocum shoveled more coal in the small stove. They had the place to themselves. The guy who ran it went off to do some business. Take an hour, he said. Slocum had bolted the door after him. Stripped down to his pants, he waited for her to finish, but in no hurry. He admired her slender body as she lathered her arms and small breasts with soap.

"You think I can drive all the way?" she asked, pausing with the bar and washcloth in her hands.

"You could drive to hell and gone."

"Good. I thought so." She smiled smuggly and resumed washing herself. "What next?"

"Food?"

"All right. Help me up?"

He reached down and with his hands under her arm pits raised her up until their faces met. Water sheeted off her skin, but he held her off her toes and kissed her. Then gently he bent over with their mouths locked until her feet could touch the floor.

"My God," she said, looking dazzled at him. "We may not be ready to eat—"

He closed off her speaking with his lips. His hand fondled the hard right breast and she pressed herself to him. The fire of need began to build in him. Her hand ran over the fly of his pants, discovering the hard ridge. In moments, her fingers fumbled with his belt and buttons, then forced his pants down.

"Sit on the bench," she breathlessly managed.

He dropped to the wooden bench. She climbed on his lap, straddling him, and soon her small hand closed on his shaft. She scooted forward on his legs until she could insert his trobbing hard-on inside her. Then, with her legs wrapped around him, she began to hunch on his pole. Her small rock-hard nipples dragged over his bare chest, and he clutched the half-moons of her butt in each hand, helping her ride.

Faster and faster, until the efforts of her muscled stomach began to close in on his manhood. Their breathing grew deeper and the room no longer existed. The cold drafts that sought them evaporated. Need began to grow and swell in the confines. A wild swirl of passion's fires consumed them, until at last, in a final charge, they both came and collapsed in each others' arms. He rocked her back and forth.

His eyelids too heavy to open, he wanted to remain there forever holding her in such contentment. Her face was buried in his shoulder, and they savored the peace of the moment.

Thirty minutes later in Rosa's Cafe, they ate a breakfast of *chorrizo* sausage, fried potatoes, scrambled eggs, and fresh flour tortillas.

"So you made it back?" Rosa said, refilling their cups.

"It wasn't easy," Slocum said, sharing a private look with Chris.

"A wonder you did not get killed out there."

"Tell me about Bruce Seaman," Slocum said, under his breath.

Rosa made a face like she was thinking. "He owns some ranches."

"What else?"

"I don't know. He is rich."

"He own the bank?"

"Oh, no, but he lives like a rich man. You know what I mean?"

"Yes, I know. He have any stagelines?"

"No, not that I know about. Why?"

"I was only asking."

"Are you looking for a new job?"

"Not today."

"Maybe you need one." Rosa shook her head and went down the counter to the other customers.

"Are we going to sleep or check on things?" Chris asked, pushing her plate away.

"We need to do both," he said, thinking over the matter. "Let's go sleep a few hours."

"Good," she said, and slapped down the money for the meal.

"I'll repay you," he said, and they headed for the front door. Rosa shouted after them to be careful, and they went outside into the chilling wind.

The Grand Hotel, the town's only two-story building, loomed on the corner a block away. Heads bent, they hurried through the swirling dust up the boardwalk. Slocum considered the saloons in passing. A few good shots of whiskey would warm him to the core. They better get some shut-eye. Maybe with some sleep his brain would clear enough to figure all this business out.

Hours later, someone rapped on their door. The sound woke Slocum, and he reached for the Colt on the dresser. How long had they slept? It was still daylight outside. His other hand stayed her in the bed under the covers.

"Yes?" He turned to listen with the grips in his fist.

"U.S. Deputy Marshal Clyde Banks."

Slocum looked at her. She nodded with a questioning frown and bounded out of bed. "I've heard of him," she hissed. In an instant, she began to dress.

"Wait till we get our clothes on," Slocum said aloud to stall the man in the hall.

"Fine," Banks said, outside the door.

He reached to pull his pants on and noticed that she was completely dressed in her boy garb. In haste, she messed up the other bed covers as if she had been sleeping in it. Satisfied that her masquerade and cover-up would work, he completed buttoning his shirt, then went and opened the door for the man.

"You must be Slocum?" the red-faced man asked. Dressed in a suit, he looked very businesslike, and nodded to Chris like he would to a stranger.

Slocum shook the lawman's hand, then showed him a seat on the straight-back chair while he sat on the edge of the bed to put on his socks and boots. The room felt cold because of a lack of central heat in the hotel. Smoothing out his first sock over his foot, Slocum looked up at the man.

"What can we do for you?"

"I'm looking for a woman, Sarah Winston, who killed a deputy U.S. Marshal in St. Louis."

"She sure ain't here." Slocum looked in Chris's direction, and she shook her head mildly as if she didn't know who he wanted.

"I know that," Banks continued. "But they told me at the stable yard that you took a passenger with you to Prescott."

"Just me and Christopher."

"Well, I'm sorry to bother you two, then."

"No problem, we needed to be up anyway." He glanced at the blowing dust outside, simply another winter day.

Banks rose and nodded to Chris as Slocum saw him to the door.

Slocum closed it, then he held his finger to his lips to silence her. He could see the rage exploding in her blue eyes, but he wanted to be certain that Banks didn't hear anything that he didn't need to.

"Easy," he said and caught her arms, when she charged across the room.

"It's all a lie!"

"How long have you known that they blamed you?" he asked, catching her in his arms.

"When he said it!" Her bewildered look convinced Slocum, she told him the truth. He released her and bent over to pull on his boots. Damn, that made it even tougher. The real killers were not even suspected, and if they killed her, no one would ever know who did it.

His boots on, he looked around the room. "I guess we better go collect some money and get ready to make a new run." He paused to offer her a chance to say no.

"Yeah, since I'm wanted too, we better get out of here."

At the stage line office, Glanding counted out the money he owed Slocum. A look of impatience on the big man's face told Slocum that the man needed the next mail on its way. But he wanted to let him suffer a little longer.

"You still driving for me?" Glanding asked.

"Yes."

"When the hell are you two going to leave?"

"Get those two buckboards loaded, then send two teams out to Maggard's today, so they're ready for us when we get there. Besides, them renegades burned Maggard's place down, so whoever you send needs to be ready for lots of trouble. We'll need fresh teams when we get there so we can push on."

"You and 'him'?" Glanding indicated her.

"Yes, we'll leave at sunup."

A look of relief spread over Glanding's ruddy face, and he sliced the perspiration off his forehead with a finger. With a wary head shake, he drew a deep breath. "I'll get it done."

"Who else wants this mail run?"

"You said something about that before." Glanding pursed his lips in deep thoughts. "Well, Ed Martin bid on it."

"Where's he at?"

"Sante Fe, I guess."

"Why do I believe this Doyle might work for him?"

"He's the one—"

"Yes, and I guess I should have shot him instead of hitting him."

"Yeah, then he'd not been back to bother us. Well, how

will we prove whether Martin hired him or not?"

"That might be hard, unless we wring Doyle's tail hard enough when we find him," Slocum said. Someone had armed the Navajo renegades, as well as paid Doyle and his bunch to snoop about the mail run's relay stations. They also had raped Chris—that recall needled him the worst.

"We're going to get some supper," Slocum said, and they left the man standing behind his desk, scowling at the pile of papers before him.

Outside the office, Slocum pulled down the brim on his Scottish cap. The cold wind whistled at the eaves of the roof; they both turned into the force of it.

"I saw a rider," she said. "He passed by while we were in the office."

"Did it look like Doyle?"

"No."

"Know him?"

"I think so. He was bundled up, but I think it was one of Vince's killers."

Slocum frowned and looked up the empty street. No sign of a rider or anyone else. "Reckon he went in the livery yard?"

"I don't know, but something about him . . ." She shook her head as if still bothered and unable to solve the issue.

He held the cafe door open for her. "Let's eat first. I'm hungry enough to gobble down a wolf."

"Don't remind me of eating dog. That dang Pearcy out there at Maggard's." She shook her head in disgust.

"Oh! You two are back again," Rosa said to them. "My candles that I burned for you weren't in vain."

"Why, they worked wonderful," Slocum said and took a seat on a stool beside Chris.

"Chili?" Rosa asked.

"Yes," they both agreed.

She poured them coffee, then went in the back to make up their food.

"What would those men be doing here?" Slocum asked her.

She shook her head.

"So, you two are going back again?" Rosa asked, bringing them their food. Two bowls of her rich, red chili and white flour tortillas on a side plate.

"Someone has to take the mail. It will be Christmas soon."

"Ah, yes, you can be Santa Claus, huh?" She looked at Slocum suspiciously.

"We hope so," Slocum said, loading his tortilla.

"You both are foolish men," she said and went back into the kitchen.

With a sly wink, Slocum elbowed Chris, and she nodded with a small grin. Then he glanced at where Rosa disappeared. Good, her disguise still worked.

Outside the cafe, Slocum put the .30 caliber in his waistband where it would be easy to reach. With Chris at his side, he headed for the livery. They reached the office in a blistering sand storm and once inside, Slocum recognized the man in charge, Lute.

"Come to get your horse?" Lute asked. A stringbean of a man, he rose from his place by the stove.

"No, I came to pay you to keep him longer."

"Fine. Howdy there, Kid. You two running together now?"

"Yes," Slocum said. "I need some information."

"What is it?"

"A man rode in here about a half-hour ago."

"You must mean Weedle."

"That's his name?"

"Calls himself that. Barstow Weedle."

"He been here long?" Slocum glanced at her, but she didn't act like she recognized the name.

"Him and Humphrey, they got here two days ago. Don't know their business. Look like drifters to me. What else you need to know?"

"How much do I owe you?" He looked at Chris again, but she shrugged again at the notion of their names. "Which one is red-headed?" Slocum asked as the man got out his lead pencil to figure the cost of keeping his horse.

"Humphrey." Lute said, busy pushing his pencil on the receipt.

She had said one of Winston's killers was red-headed. Slocum shared a confidential nod with her.

Slocum paid the bill on his horse, and they left his office. On the porch, he turned to her. He didn't need them by chance recognizing her even if she was dressed like a boy.

"They don't know me. You go back to the hotel room and wait for me. I'm going to scout them out back there." He indicated the bunk house in the back of the yard.

"Be careful," she said, sounding concerned.

"Always." He watched her reluctantly leave and head down the boardwalk for the hotel. When he was satisfied she was on her way, he crossed the yard for the bunk house. A wave of dust swept up from the street spun around him. He let it subside, then he pushed his way inside the bunk room's door. His eyes adjusted to the dark interior's lamplight. A red-head sat up on a bottom bunk. He wore a full red beard, and appeared half-awake with his blind white eyeball.

"Looking for someone?" Humphrey asked gruffly.

"Might be."

"Yeah, well what is it?"

"A guy in Sante Fe was supposed to send me some money."

"Well, we damn sure ain't got it," the second one said and raised up in the upper bunk. "What was his name?"

"Fine," Slocum said, acting satisfied and turned on his heel.

"Didn't catch your name," Weedle demanded.

"Didn't give it." And Slocum went outside. He needed them separated and both drunk. Where was that marshal? Would he listen to him? He needed more details of the murder from Chris. Those two were dug in as if they were waiting for something. How would he ever pull this off?

First, he needed all the details about the killing. Every one of them, then he'd find that marshal. Hurrying against the sharp wind, he pushed for the hotel. He mounted the stairs and took them two at a time.

He rapped on the door of their room.

"Slocum?"

"Yes."

"Oh, thank God," she said and hugged him. "I was so worried."

"I'm fine. They're over there, but we've got to go over this killing again."

"What can we do about them?"

"I'm trying to figure it out." He looked over her shoulder and watched two riders in the street, headed west, leading two loose teams. Good, Glanding was doing his part.

14

Slocum found Marshal Banks standing at the bar in the
Elephant Saloon. The man was hoisting a mug of beer
when he came inside the barroom. He went to join him
and took his poncho off over his head. After it was off,
he replaced his cap.

"I'll buy you a beer," the lawman said.

"I'll take one," Slocum said. He set the blanket on the
bar and hitched his own gun in place.

The handlebar-mustached bartender delivered it. Slocum nodded to the man and then turned to Banks. "Let's
go over in the corner, we have things to discuss."

"Fine, I was about to head back on the stage for Sante
Fe. All my leads here on that woman Sarah Winston have
expired." They slipped in the booth, sitting opposite each
other.

"What if I knew who killed Vincent?" Slocum put his
folded poncho on the seat beside him.

"You know where to find her?"

"I know where the two killers are at this minute."

"Wait, you say killers?"

"The two men who killed Vincent Winston are at the
livery yard."

"You must know where she is then?"

"Lower your voice," Slocum said and looked around to be certain they hadn't drawn any attention.

"If you are harboring her—"

"Two men, not his wife, stabbed Vincent in an alley behind The Moose Head Saloon."

"Who are they? Besides, she was never his wife." Like a fussy old woman, Banks dismissed her marital status with a head shake of disapproval.

"It wasn't her."

"Who did you say were the killers?"

"One calls himself Humphrey, he has red hair and one eye. The other has black hair. His name is Weedle."

"You say, I mean, she says that they killed Vincent?"

"Right." Slocum tried to keep down his edge of impatience with the man.

"Can she prove it?"

"She can testify."

"Her word against theirs."

"She's willing to risk facing them down, while you listen in."

"That could be dangerous."

"I have a plan. Here's how we do it. They're over in the livery bunkhouse. I'm going in there first and throw my bedroll down like I'm staying. Then she comes in and gets the drop on them. You can listen at the doorway. I'll back her if it gets too bad."

"She really thinks they'll confess when she confronts them?"

Slocum nodded and took his first sip of beer. Maybe he had the man willing to listen. It was a big risk. Anything could go wrong, but Chris felt strong enough to give it a try. If it didn't work, Banks would arrest her. The man had little more ambition than to do much more than take her in.

"You willing?"

"I could arrest her—"

"You could shit, too."

"You threatening an officer—"

"Banks, let's say, either you listen to this or let the killers of Vince Winston off scot-free."

"All right, but it better not be a trick."

Slocum wanted to say that for two bits he'd bust him over the head and drag his worthless carcass out in the alley to freeze. But he bit back the words. "It ain't a trick, but open your ears when she goes inside that room."

He left the saloon still not satisfied; Banks was hardly more than a warrant server. Still if his plan worked, it would clear her of the charges. If Banks didn't do something foolish—lots of if's in the deal.

On the way to the yard, Slocum took his bedroll from the buckboard, which he figured was enough to carry inside and relieve their suspicions that he was a only a new occupant of the bunkhouse. He headed for where he planned to meet Chris and Banks out of the sight of the pair in the bunkhouse.

He arrived first, and Banks came huddling in his light coat, stomping his feet. He grumbled about the cold and where was she? He didn't look up when she joined them.

"Christine, this is Marshal Banks," Slocum said as they stood in the space between the mercantile and harness shop.

"Him? I mean her?" Banks raised his eyebrows in disbelief and used his right arm to hold on to his bowler in the wind gusts.

"It's her." Slocum made an impatient frown to settle the man. They had a deal and he wasn't getting out of it. "Now, I'm going over there. Give me about ten minutes to get settled. If I figure it won't work, I'll come back out in a few minutes."

Banks made an impatient look at her.

"You listening?" Slocum demanded.

"This better work."

"Banks! Don't threaten me or her. We're trying to find you two killers. You listen good, hear me?"

Banks agreed, but his attitude didn't satisfy Slocum. He told Chris to be careful and went across the street with his roll on his shoulder. The sharp wind seared his eyes and the dust made him blink.

He pushed his way in the bunk room. Humphrey looked up from his game of solitaire.

"You back?" he asked, then turned back to search the cards on the small table.

"Yeah, that guy's got my money ain't here yet, I guess." Slocum tossed his bedroll on a top bunk.

"Yeah," Humphrey said, busy with his cards. "He owes you very much he may never come. May hightail with it."

Slocum nodded. Weedle was behind a dog-eared Police Gazette, leaning back in a straight-back chair. He gave Slocum a cold-fish look and went back to his reading.

"Damn. Is there a fire in that stove?" Slocum asked with a frown.

"Hell, I've stoked it a dozen times," Weedle complained.

Slocum spread his bedroll and then undid his gun belt, wrapped it up, and set it on the bed. He took off his boots and climbed up to get under the covers like he sought someplace warm.

"Wake me up for supper," he said, climbed in the upper bunk, and pulled the covers over him. Careful to hide his actions, he slid the Colt out of the holster and grasped it in his hand. It was up to Chris next. He hoped Banks had good ears.

Time clicked away slowly. He listened to the whistle of the wind at the roof eaves. This could be a tough situation, unless—no time for regrets, they were committed.

He heard the door creak on the hinges. He waited on his back, his heart throbbing hard under his rib cage. Ready to spring into action, he listened for her words.

"Got a new customer," Humphrey said.

"Yeah, place is getting damn crowded," Weedle said from behind the magazine.

"I won't be long," Chris said. "Get your hands up. You're the ones killed Marshall Vincent—"

"Huh! Who the hell are you—" Weedle's voice ran

down at the sight of the sheriff's model pistol in her fist.

"Listen, Kid," Humphrey said, getting to his feet. "Who said we shot him?"

"I never said you shot him. Said you killed him. Stabbed him to death."

"Shut up!" Weedle ordered his partner, taking charge. "He's bluffing."

"I saw you two knife him down in the alley behind the Moose Head Saloon."

"Then you must be his bitch!" Humphrey said, at his discovery.

"I saw you two do it."

"What the hell you going to do about it?" Weedle shouted in a rage.

"Don't—" Slocum shouted and rolled over on the bunk, pointing the cocked Colt at him.

Weedle tried to draw. Chris's revolver belched smoke, flame, and fire. The acrid blue cloud billowed inside the room. It blurred Slocum's vision. Her bullet threw Weedle over backwards and he began to scream. Banks burst in the front door and Humphrey flashed out the back one in the smoky confusion.

"He's getting away!" Slocum shouted to the lawman.

"I know," Banks shouted and hurried past Chris, holding his gun ready and going around the upset table. He hung out the back door, but Slocum knew by the way he looked in both directions that Humphrey was gone. He eased off the bed and jerked Weedle to his feet.

"Why did you kill him?" Slocum demanded in the moaning man's face.

"I'm dying," Weedle cried.

"You want a doctor, then talk."

"He—"

"Who?"

"Vincent, he sent my brother up for counterfeiting. We figured he'd get us next."

"Enough for you?" Slocum shouted to Banks, still in the doorway, checking his pistol.

"I heard him. Sorry," he said to Chris, who stood pale-faced with the smoking Colt still hanging in the hand at her side.

"I need a doctor," Weedle cried.

"You need a hangman," Banks said and jerked him by the collar over to a chair. "You two killed Marshal Vincent?"

"I said so."

Banks straightened and holstered his gun. He turned to Chris. "Words ain't worth much, Missy, but I'll see that warrant for you is withdrawn."

She shoved the six shooter in the holster and nodded. Slocum had his bedroll gathered. He turned back to the lawman. "Guess you'll catch Humphrey."

"He can't go far. And thanks, Slocum. I owe you one."

"Good. I'll save it for when I need it. This part's over for us, we've got mail to haul." He motioned to the doorway.

"Gawd amighty!" Lute burst in. "What's happening out here?"

"Marshal Banks tried to capture a couple of killers," Slocum said and nodded to the lawman. He saw the local law and several more coming. He gave a head swing for her to go ahead; he didn't want to be interrogated all day about it. Let Banks explain it to them. They stood back as the others came inside.

"U.S. Deputy Marshal—" Banks began, and Slocum and Chris skirted them and left the bunkhouse porch.

"How far do you reckon Humphrey's got?" she asked, looking back over her shoulder, then turning back beside him.

"If he got a horse, he's halfway to the Arizona line already."

"If not, he's still here," she said, looking about suspiciously as they plied the boardwalk to the hotel.

"You can worry about stuff like that till you're sick."

"You don't figure he's a grizzly bear, huh?"

"Just a cheap back-shooter." He smiled down at her to relieve her concern.

"Where's Doyle?" she asked under her breath as they swept into the hotel.

"Hiding under a cowpaddy somewhere."

"He out west of here?" She motioned in that direction.

He looked up the stairs, prepared to go up to their room. Then he dropped his gaze. "Probably." And went up the steps, herding her ahead of him.

15

The dawn was still wrapped up in the cold night, when
she clucked to her horses and, handily wheeling them,
sent them out the gate of the stageline yard in a whirl of
dust. Slocum nodded to the concerned-faced Glanding
standing in the lamplight on the dock. No time for more
words, he sent his horses off in her wake. The starlight
bathed the empty street in a dim, pearly illumination. His
fresh team charged the bits, and it felt good to be on the
move again. How much longer he could make these trips
depended. Depended on when the Abbott brothers discovered his existence there. Someone would wire them, word
would leak out, and the Kansas deputies would arrive.
That he saw them first was all he worried about.

His thoughts of the supple body of Christine in bed
warmed him. The woolen muffler was waving over his
shoulder, the Scottish cap pulled down. He could see her
wearing the new cap he bought her. A cowboy hat would
freeze one's brains to death in these low temperatures.
Strange that so early in the winter this frigid temperature
persisted. Usually a warm wind swept up out of old Mexico and warmed things up a few days between cold snaps.
Those warm spots must be down there dancing with some

pretty señoritas at a *fandango*. He slapped the ponies and they hit the up-grade on Chris's heels.

A purple light spread over the red bluff tops to the north of them as the sun tried to light the cavernous night. Filled with pride at Chris's expert driving, he glanced back. Word was out. They learned at breakfast that Humphrey managed to steal a horse and left for parts unknown. No one had seen Doyle either. Slocum wondered if the outlaw was somewhere west of them or had fled, figuring he was wanted for rape and other high crimes. He shook his head; no telling where that no-account had gone.

They drew up on a mesa and let the horses blow. She went to the right, he turned left. He studied the scattered junipers and brown grass. Nothing out of place. She soon rejoined him.

"Enjoying it?" he asked, seeing the gleam in her blue eyes.

"Yeah, more than I thought I would," she said, clutching his arm with an expression of excitement. "You know, I never figured I would get Vincent's killers. And we got one of them and identified the other one."

"The U.S. marshals will get him in time."

"Glad they're not out looking for me anymore."

Slocum nodded, his mind on their relief horses that were sent to Maggard's. They would need them, pushing the teams this hard. He recalled seeing them headed up there. Glanding promised him the two men who took them to the line were tough enough. Navajo renegades—no word that the army hadn't stopped them yet. It was still going to be a helluva trip.

"We better get on our way." He glanced down, and she was on her toes. He kissed her.

"A warm bath and bed?" she asked.

"In Preskitt," he said and grinned back at her. "Just don't count on sleeping much."

"Ha." Then she poked him in the gut with her gloved hand, turned, and ran to climb onto her buckboard. She waved to him and took her seat. In a wink, she headed west with her team. Pleased with her, he sent his after her's.

In midafternoon, he took the lead position on the last few miles to the Maggard turn off. He saw horses and men waiting ahead. Standing up, he reined in his team, and she pulled her lathered, hard-blowing horses alongside his.

"What is it?"

"They're waiting up there at the turnoff. Looks all right. You stay here. I'll be certain."

"You be careful," she said.

With a nod, he set his team off at a trot. Then, after advancing, and now holding them back, he studied everything about the horses and men for any sign of a trap. It could be, and he didn't need any trouble with two rigs. For certain they required the fresh animals; they had pushed their teams hard this far.

One of the men came out. Slocum uncovered his gun from all the clothes and swung the horses around.

"Señor Slocum, you are here!" the man said, looking relieved.

"Yes." On his feet, Slocum fought the hard-breathing team down.

"Maggard's is burned out." The man tossed his head in that direction.

"Yes, I told Glanding that. What will we do for fresh horses here when I come back?"

The Mexican man turned to his partner who joined them, and they looked uncertain.

"You tell Glanding to have two fresh teams here in six days for our return."

"*Si*, we do that." The older man acted relieved and his partner joined his head in bobbing agreement to the terms.

"Let's trade teams," he said and waved her in.

"We can do that," the man assured him.

"Good," he said and went to lift the tarp. They'd have some jerky and cheese, washed down with barrel water. Guess it beat dog stew, anyway.

"They kill anyone up there?" Slocum asked the older man who understood English.

"We didn't look too close," the man said, obviously extremely nervous from waiting out there all night and half the day for their arrival.

"Reckon they killed Pearcy?" she asked.

"Yeah, and they probably ate his dog meat," Slocum said as she stared across the rolling country.

"Figure those renegades did it?" she asked, pulling off her gloves and then taking some jerky from him.

"I guess. From here on we better keep our eyes open. It will be long past dark when we make the trading post." He chewed thoughtfully as the two changed the harness expertly to the fresh team.

"We sleeping there?"

"Four hours or so. Then we better push on."

She nodded, and chewed on the dried meat. At last, she spoke. "You aim to be back in seven days."

"Yes, we can do it."

"Be a challenge."

"If all this riffraff leaves us alone, we can do it."

"You figure this Dog Shit is going to try to stop us?"

"If he knows we're out here, yes."

"Let's pray he don't know it."

"There's a good chance he has scouts watching the road for buckboards."

"You still don't consider him a grizzly?"

"No, just a yapping dog."

"Why can't the army round him up?"

Slocum shook his head. "That's a big question. They don't have a great record at doing such things. We better get heading for the Little Colorado."

She took off running for her rig. Taking the lines, she bound onto the seat, turned to wait for his nod, and then was off.

"*Muchas gracias,*" Slocum said to the pair and gave his horses the bits. With a wave to them, he knew the nervous pair would race back to the security of Fort Wingate. Couldn't blame them, tangling with renegades wasn't that interesting anyway. He slapped his ponies to catch up, she was out-distancing him.

Wind in his face again, wheel rims singing, and the horses stretched out in a hard run, he felt grateful for the sun's growing warmth. Maybe the south wind hadn't forgotten them. He'd be glad when the *fandango* was over down there. A glance to the left and he studied the purple, distant range edging that end of the world. He hoped his ambitious plans for the mail run weren't too much for his partner. He glanced ahead and appraised the distance to catch her, and slapped them to go faster. He was getting behind.

Carried by the wind, small wisps of dust from her wheels fled to the north. He drove his team and saw her point in that direction. He rose to his feet and squinted to better see what she meant. Then he spotted the rider in a grove of junipers. Was it one of Dog Shit's lookouts? Time would tell, but a heavy rock formed in the bottom of his belly when the rider turned off and disappeared.

Slocum nodded hard to her that he saw him. Damn. Well at least they had some warning. Dog Shit would have to burn some saddle leather to catch them. Time that scout got back to them and they got mounted. It might be after they stopped at the trading post—they would need that sleep. They'd both be wiped out by then. No, he wasn't changing his plans for those worthless louse-eaters. But he would have some fireworks ready for them if they tried him. Yes, he'd have that ready.

They took a breather with the dying red sun out over the far horizon. Chewing on some dried apple slices and crackers, they let the hard-pushed animals stomp out some of their discomfort.

"You think that was one of his men?"

Slocum looked back down the empty tracks. "Yeah, more than likely, but their old ponies couldn't keep up with these fresh horses. I figure they'll try us when we leave the trading post in the morning."

"What will we do about them?"

"Give them what for," he said, between sips of cold barrel water from a tin cup.

"Can you light and throw them and drive?" Her eyes narrowed in disbelief.

"Guess I better learn how," he said and laughed.

She drove a fiended fist into his gut. "Be serious."

"I am. They try us, we'll blow their heads off."

She looked at the sky for help. He reached out and hugged her shoulder. "I been thinking a lot harder about that hot bath and hotel bed in Preskitt than them renegades."

"Hope we get there to enjoy it," she said and warily inhaled.

16

"Señor Slocum!" Pasquel shouted, coming out onto the porch in the lamplight. His next words in Spanish called the boys to take the lathered spent teams and wagons away.

"Ah, you have two rigs this time," Pasquel said, shaking Slocum's firm hand.

"Christmas mail," Slocum said. He looked over as Chris about stumbled on her way toward them. It concerned him that she might be too tired.

"We'll sleep a few hours and be ready to head out."

"Ah, yes. You got fresh horses at Maggard's this time?"

"Maggard's was burned out, but Glanding had fresh horses there for us."

"Burned out?"

Slocum nodded and turned to her. "You all right, partner?"

Obviously done in, she looked at him out of sleepy eyes.

"You two need some food?" Pasquel asked.

"No. Sleep," she mumbled.

"Go ahead. That same room is yours."

"Get us up at dawn," Slocum said.

"Not before?" she asked him.

"No, we'll need daylight leaving here."

"Yeah," she agreed numbly, and Slocum brought their bedrolls, herding her on.

They shed only their coats and boots, climbed into their blankets, and dropped fast asleep.

Slocum awoke to the knocking at their door. "We're awake," he said to the knocker and sat up.

"You may be," she said. "I'm not." With one hand, she swept her short hair back and glared at him in the room's dim light. "Time, ain't it?"

"Time for lots of things. Mostly grabbing some real grub and heading out."

She agreed in defeat, and they pulled on their boots with groans. Bedrolls under their arms, they went to the kitchen area. A smiling Mexican woman served them heaping platters, showed them a table, and poured them coffee in pottery cups.

Pasquel, looking sleepy-eyed, joined them. "So they burned out Maggard's. Who did that?"

"I figure Dog Shit and his renegades," Slocum said, looking up from using his flour tortilla to scoop up beans, eggs, and pork.

"That one is bad."

"No, he ain't bad, he's worthless, and the army needs to run him down with some tough Indian scouts."

"All them are down south with General Crook after the Apaches."

"They need to get about a handful to come up here. A few days and they would have the renegades in chains or buzzard bait. Does Dog Shit come here?"

"No, he caused trouble once. I banned him from ever coming back. But he robs the poor families after they leave here, and I can't stop him."

"Not your job. The army needs some prodding on him and his bunch."

"He will get stronger."

Slocum agreed, lifting his cup for a sip of the rich brew. "Yes, more young bucks will join him. Especially since he got the repeaters and ammunition."

Pasquel agreed.

Before they left, Slocum took time to load six sticks and set them in a small wooden box that he tied in place on the floor beside his right boot. Pasquel watched with interest.

"What will you do with them?"

"Give them a Chinese New Year, if they try us."

The man shook his head and drew in a deep breath. "Looks very dangerous."

"It is if I light one and it goes off. Ready Chris?"

She nodded, and ran for her rig. Beaming in the early golden light, she stood with the reins in her hands, awaiting his nod.

Pasquel gave him a "good luck" shout and stood back. Slocum looked at her and bobbed his chin with a grin to signal go. *Give'em hell, girl.*

They left the trading post in a great circle. Rims digging up a fine spray of dust, the wagons headed west. Beside Slocum's foot, his arsenal rode. His shirt pocket bulged with gopher matches. They struck out down the willow-lined Little Colorado. Far in the west, some high mountains like small mounds marked their way.

Slocum looked back as the man and his waving assistants became smaller by the minute. He turned back to his driving. Was that worthless renegade and his boys ahead of them? If they were, he intended to blow them away. This time he'd not be so stingy with Glanding's explosives.

The horses flattened out in a gallop and he kept his team within twenty yards of her tailgate. It gave him more dust in his face at this distance, but he wanted to be close to her in case anything happened. Were those rengades hiding in the willows ahead? Perhaps they'd attack them where they'd be forced to pull their animals down to a trot on the steep places? He shook his head; it would be whenever they wanted to easily get at them, and certainly not up to him.

The rise ahead meant they must slow down. The road

widened and he drove his horses up beside hers. She glanced over and nodded.

"In case they're up there, let me go first. They start attacking, I want you to get the hell out of here."

"I ain't leaving you!" she shouted back.

"Hell, girl, do as I say," he said above the horses and wagons' rumble.

"Go on," she said. "I'm backing you."

He shook his head in disapproval and drove his rig past her. He scoured the grassland as the road parted from the river and took to the knoll. Then he saw them. First unblocked hats, then calico ponies. They carried rifles and were waiting. Their chances of hitting a bull in the butt while riding horseback and shooting those rifles were slim. At closer range, the odds increased, still he needed to be—then he recalled her, stood up, looked back, and nodded that they were going to charge the line.

At the base of the hill, he switched the reins to his left hand and went for his matches with the right. Scratching them two at a time, he finally had a long fuse sputtering. Then he lit another. Half distracted, jolted on the seat, he manged to light two more. Then he took the reins and began to scream like a banshee at the bays. He charged the team at them.

He saw their distrust begin when they milled their ponies about. Then he reached down and grasped a stick of the blasting powder in his right hand. He tossed it wide right.

Still screaming, he could hear her voice joining his. The rengades recalled the blasting sticks and bolted their horses away. In the mass confusion, Dog Shit fired his rifle. The muzzle puffed a cloud of smoke. Then the first stick blew up and sent Slocum's team into a fly. He managed to throw the last one as he watched the spooked paint under Dog Shit leave off bucking through the juniper brush.

Chris came charging around on his left side, shouting, "We did it!"

He nodded in approval and slapped his ponies to follow

behind her. On the rise, he turned on the seat and saw the disgusted-looking renegades gathering up. They could never catch the grain-fed horses.

But there would be another day. The matter would never be settled by merely scattering them. He could only hope the army did their part and soon. They would be at Kay McNeal's place for fresh teams by midafternoon. He glanced back. No pursuit.

"Damn, oh damn, Slocum, you sure pushed them ponies," Kay said, standing with her hand to shade her eyes from the high sun.

"We've got mail to deliver," he said. "Besides, we've been chased by them damn renegades."

"They're still pestering folks?"

"They tried back there twenty miles."

"Someone needs to cut that damn Dog Shit. Then stick his leg down through his bag and let him hobble around. Then he wouldn't bother so many God-fearing folks." She shook her head, and they began to unharness his sweaty team.

"That would be one cure," Slocum said.

"You making it this time in a week?" she asked.

"Trying."

"Maggard have your horses ready this time?" she asked, setting off the harness.

"Burned out. Guess they killed Pearcy."

"Oh, Lord, who did that?"

"Damned if I know. Glanding had our fresh horses out there on the Arizona line for us so we made that all right."

"Who do you reckon killed Pearcy?"

"Can't say, Kay. Glanding's Mexicans with horses met us on the road. We never saw the place, except at night, on our way back and we didn't stay long. I thought the army had taken care of the attackers."

"Hell fire, them worthless soldiers couldn't wipe their backsides, let alone catch renegades. You expect too much, Slocum."

"Well, I expect to be at Isaac Denton's by midnight, so we get these horses changed."

"You're a killer. Poor girl will quit you, you work her that hard for very long."

"Naw," Slocum drawled, seeing her coming back from the facilities. "She eats road dust real good."

Kay agreed with a nod, and they started for the other team. Soon stripped of the harness, the sweat soaked animals were left standing as the three went for the fresh ones. The job took less than ten minutes, and then they were eating some of Kay's fried-apple-pie and swigging down her coffee beside the rigs.

"I sure hope to hell that them folks in Preskitt appreciate their Christmas mail getting there."

Chris nodded between bites. "Oh they will, ma'am. They really will."

"Ha, folks never appreciate it, just bitch when it don't work."

"Kay," Slocum said and hugged her shoulder. "Keep your Winchester loaded to the gate and don't take no chances. They burned down one station, you could be next."

"I'd like them to try." Her brown eyes narrowed with hard indignation.

"Don't take chances," he cautioned.

She relented and nodded. "You two keep your butts on them seats and don't get off that old road in the dark."

"We won't," Slocum promised. He watched Chris take her place and nodded for her to go ahead. Reins in his hands, he smiled at the woman.

"Kay, you be on your toes. That worthless renegade is out there somewhere."

"He comes here, he'll be awishing he hadn't."

Slocum stepped up and took his place and nodded to Chris. She clucked to the team, slapped them, and left Kay McNeal's in a high run.

"See you!" Kay shouted.

He nodded and sent his ponies after Chris's disappearing dust streak. Damn, he would be glad to be at Isaac

Denton's. Watching the sun drop toward the horizon to his right, the rigs' iron rims churned up the dirt of the road. They would make it in three days at this rate. Four hours sleep at Denton's, then drop over the rim. He felt confident chasing his partner, who disappeared over the rise and then came into view when he topped the next high point. Urging his team on, he felt filled with a new-found strength. They'd soon be in Preskitt on schedule.

A smile crossed his sun-cracked lips. Hot bath and a room and a bed full of her—whew.

Denton's dogs barking broke the star-studded night. Colt in one hand, lamp in the other, the rancher came out and shouted to them.

"Two wagons. Damn, you two are becoming a regular wagon train."

"Good to see you. We're taking a few hours sleep. Wake us before dawn," Slocum said, unhitching the single trees from the outside horse.

"Go to bed in there. Glanding's paying me to take care and change these horses."

"You're super," Slocum said, digging out the bedroll.

"You seen him since you were here?"

"Doyle?"

"Yeah."

"No, he's disappeared."

"I'd like to find him," Denton said through his teeth. Then he took off his hat for her.

"Put it back on, Isaac, I'm still that 'boy,' " she said.

"Ma'am, I sure don't think so." Denton hustled off to care for the deep-breathing horses.

"I heard him say we were supposed to go sleep?" she asked, standing unsteady in her boots.

"He said it. He's taking care of the stock." Slocum handed her the bedroll.

"God bless him, and don't wake me up."

"I won't for four hours," Slocum said after her as she headed for the house.

"Get us up in four hours," Slocum reminded him and followed her.

Numb to the core, he knew this time they could safely sleep on the floor of the rancher's cabin. Morning would come early enough and then they'd drop over the rim. Two days gone and the third should put them in Preskitt. It would be a seven-day turnaround this time if all went well.

The rattle of coffee cups and the smell of bacon cooking woke Slocum. He nodded to the man busy stirring about the room, then went outside and relieved himself. Rubbing his shirt sleeves to warm them from the chill of the predawn, he returned inside.

"Been cold about long enough," he said to Denton. Then he knelt and shook her awake.

"Oh, no," she groaned. "I could sleep a week here on this soft floor."

"We ain't got a week."

"I know." She threw back the covers and shook out her boot to pull it on. "But I can complain, can't I?"

"All you want. Better wear a coat out there. The stove's off again."

"Isaac! You don't have any hot air piped out there yet?" she asked.

"No ma'am, but there will be if you stop here very often."

She grinned and shook her head. "I can't promise nothing. I'm working for him."

"Tough boss too," Denton said and poured Slocum some coffee.

"You two plotting against me?" Slocum asked.

"Naw," she said, shrugging on her coat and pushing her hands out of the sleeves. "But you sure like to get things done on time."

They laughed as she went outside.

The sun creased a flannel sky when they hee-yahed their teams out of the cowboy's yard. Slocum took the lead and they swilled up road dust in their wake. He felt more comfortable by the hour as he found the snow retreated to the eternal shade of the pinons, ponderosas, and rocks. The narrow road sections dried by the sun, they descended into the Verde Valley watching the sun set over the towering mountains in the west.

They'd be at Thorpe's before the twilight played out. He turned to see that she was right behind him. Seeing her beaming with enthusiasm, he felt renewed. Turning back, he set his team into a gallop again. The Preskitt mail was coming through.

"Damned if you ain't got two buckboards," Thorpe said as he came outside to view them. He ran his hands under his gallouses and nodded in approval. "Glanding ought to be busting his buttons."

"He should be. How quick can we get a change?" Slocum asked.

"Go in and get some food, we'll have you ready in fifteen minutes."

"Hear that Chris?"

"Yes, and I could eat a bear," she said, and quickly tied off and jumped down to join him.

"Make it a grizzly," Slocum said and laughed at his own joke. Then he shed his poncho, for the warmth of the valley had him wanting to do it for miles. They headed together for the open, lighted doorway.

The rich smell of food about bowled him over. Thorpe's woman showed them to a table and soon began to fill the table with dishes.

"We've got that mountain to make," Chris said under her breath, and motioned to the ceiling.

"No avalanche this time," he promised her.

"I've been dreading that dang mountain up there all the time. It sure was steep."

"Want me to hang a lamp on my tailgate to show you the way?"

"That might help. That canyon was so dark—" Her shoulders gave a tremble under the shirt.

"Hey, we've been through worse hell to get here."

She looked up and forced a smile. "I know, there's a hot bath and a warm bed ahead."

He dropped his gaze to the plate of food before him. "And remember, damn little sleep."

She chuckled quietly, then nodded and went back to cutting her meat. "I heard you."

"So you did." He felt better than he had in days. The mountain would be no small task in the starlight, but he could already smell the turpentine-piney smells of the upper reaches of the pass.

Four hours later, he walked his hard-breathing team and could see the outline of thumb butte west of Prescott. He stood up and waved his hat. There below them were lights of the territorial capitol. He clucked to the horses and they took the down-grade at a strong trot. Behind him, he could hear her telling her animals the barn was just ahead. It drew a grin on his mouth, now bristled with whiskers.

The clock struck one A.M. when the hotel desk clerk rushed about to get the hot water hauled to their room. Slocum helped the sleepy lad haul the copper tub upstairs. Then with the basin filled and with a reserve number of buckets to rinse with, he closed the door behind him.

"Don't spill a lot on the floor," the clerk cautioned from behind it. "It'll leak on the customers downstairs. They'll sure complain."

"We won't," Slocum said and turned the key in the lock.

He turned to watch her shed her pants, the snowy legs kicking them free. Then she stripped off the shirt and the small pear-shaped mounds escaped the underwear top. Out of it, she wet her lips and came on her toes across the room to the steaming tub.

"I could jump in it," she said.

"The splash might drown our neighbors downstairs," he said, taking off his socks and shaking them out while he watched the shapely turn of her long hip. His tiredness fled like a pinc-log fire stirred up with a poker. He could imagine running his calloused palm over the smoothness of her skin. Stripped down to his pants, he filled the pitcher with hot water and took a last look at her nudity outside the water. Then he took the vessel to the dresser. His face soon soaped, he listened as she sung a song about the wild prairie flowers. Then he stropped the razor a few times and began to shave away the wiry growth.

"Where did you learn that?" he asked, leaning over to the smoky mirror for the close work around his mouth.

"A girl lived near us in St. Louis sang it."

"She had seen them, hadn't she?"

"She made two wagon trips to California. Both tragic ones for her, but she still sang of them."

He nodded. The job of shaving about over, he wet the corner of a towel to mop the traces from the tight, smooth skin. At last completed, he slipped out of his pants and underwear. She was out of the tub drying, her arched back like that of a marble statue of a nude he once saw in a rich man's plantation house as a boy growing up in Alabama.

"You getting in?" she asked and glanced back at the tub.

"Yes, ma'am, I have about ten tons of dust I'd like to get shed of."

She dried her short hair and nodded in approval. "I'll be under the covers. This room is getting colder."

"It won't be long."

"I'm counting on it."

"What's that?"

"The lack of sleep."

The warm water closing around him, he smiled at her words. He had big plans. But the bath came first. At last completed, he rinsed himself off with a luke-warm bucket and stepped out to dry. Despite the hour he felt revived and, briskly drying himself, he considered her arranging the covers over her.

"About time," she said in a husky voice and held out her arms for him.

He slid into her hug, and the warmth radiated from her smooth skin like a heating stove. Flesh to flesh, he sought her mouth, her neck, her rock-hard nipples until she tossed under his kneading hands with a growing need for him. She raised his face to pull him on top.

His hips ached to hump against her. Soon he overcame the tangle of their legs to mount her, and his throbbing manhood sought her. He entered the silky tight entrance and closed his eyes to the sheer ectasy of the moment. She cried out loud, and her fingers clutched his shoulders. He wondered if their sleeping neighbors, below and aside, had awakened to her sounds of pleasure. The notion was only a fleeting one, for he savored the depth of her mine, driving deeper and deeper, his force met by her muscular stomach. The tempo increased. Soon the ropes under the mattress began to noisily protest their fury.

Her small legs wrapped tight around him and her heels dug into the backs of his legs. In the starlight that filtered into the window, he could see her tossing her head in wild abandonment on the pillow. Her actions only stirred him to greater involvement. Spasms of her contraction began to encircle his taunt shaft, and her moans increased. At last, from the depth of his scrotum sharp lightning pains struck his testicles. The flow rose like a volcanic explosion, it began to fill the tubes, pushed hard by his efforts up the circular route, and then finally was forced out, spewing with a blinding force that split the glan wide open. She clutched him, shoved her belly hard against him, threw her head back and cried out, "Oh, yes." It lasted for a long time, depleting them of all their strength.

They fell in a pile and slept until the sun's golden rays found them. Then, savoring their closeness and body warmth, they snuggled together and went back to sleep some more.

17

They ate breakfast in the diner. Slocum's eyelids still felt lead-weighted. The reporter from the Daily Miner, busy taking notes with his pencil, looked up. His youthful face glowed with enthusiasm.

"How did you two ever manage to get two mail wagons through?"

Slocum looked over at Chris, who was busy eating and saying little. He turned back to the youth. "Mr. Glanding said he needed the mail delivered. There had been some real bad deals. Three men were killed earlier trying to get it through. That meant there weren't lots of folks who were willing to drive the wagon."

"Yes, but you've got through twice now."

"Pure luck."

"They say at the livery that you carry fused sticks of blasting powder on the rig with you?"

"Oh, we have some."

"You ever have to use them?" The boy's green eyes widened and his pencil stood poised as he waited for the reply.

"It's a good enforcer."

"Enforcer?"

Slocum raised the coffee cup and nodded to emphasize

his meaning. He took a sip of the rich brew and he put the cup down.

"Takes lots of starch out of folks bent on stopping you to receive one of them sputtering like a personal letter. It sure gets results."

"Oh, I bet it does. How often have you used them?"

Slocum cut up his ham before he looked up at the boy. "Quite frequently, until they got the message."

"You ever blow up any of them outlaws?"

"Don't know, didn't stay around to look for the pieces." He busied himself eating the ham. Chewing thoughtfully, he let the boy sit on the edge of his chair before he continued. "We kept on driving, but those highway men didn't bother us again."

"Yeah, they got the message," the boy said and grinned as if he had solved a great mystery. "Mister Slocum, you and Chris are sure doing this city a big service. I hope folks appreciate it. I'm going to tell them in the next edition too."

"Have a good day," Slocum said and waved him away with his fork.

"You too," the boy said and rushed off with his notes.

Chris looked up to be certain the reporter was out of earshot, then she spoke under her breath, "They'll be calling you Blaster after this."

"Been called worse," he said, swabbing up the last traces of his breakfast with a slab of sourdough bread.

"When we heading back?"

"Soon as we get the teams hitched."

"Ain't no grass growing under your feet," she said wryly and pushed her plate away.

"You got anything you want to do here?"

She shook her head and rose with him. He paid the waitress at the front end of the counter. She nodded her approval and added how she appreciated the letters they brought in.

"Keep up the good work," she said after them.

"Some folks appreciate us," Chris said, outside in the warming sun.

"Yeah, some do. Say it may thaw out today. I think it will." Slocum removed his cap and put up the flaps.

They walked the block to the livery. The assistant named Joshua smiled when they came in the office. Seated before the large desk piled with receipts and notices, he swiveled around and nodded to both of them.

"Boss said you'd be itching to head back."

"They bring down the mail?" Slocum asked, dropping on a straight-back chair.

"We've already got it loaded and tarped down. Even refilled your water barrel." The younger man beamed with his arms crossed over his chest and nodded confidently.

"Sounds like we need horses hitched."

"They're harnessed and waiting."

"You're a good man, Josh. I'll put in for a raise for you," Slocum said with private look at Chris that he was ready.

She agreed and they headed for the alleyway. The help brought out the two teams and in minutes they were hitched. Slocum stood aside with her for a few words.

"We could have some trouble, you realize, going back?"

"I know," she said softly.

"Reckon you can handle it?"

"Why?" She looked up with a frown.

"We could take one back."

"Not on your life. I can haul my own freight in this deal."

Slocum hunched his shoulders, regretting he had even asked. Lord, he only wanted her safe. He exhaled and nodded.

"Then get your butt up on that seat, daylight's burning."

"That's better," she said, then flew up on the buckboard, gathering lines and looking smug.

"*Muchas gracias,*" he said to the Mexican help, took his reins, and climbed up. He nodded for her to start off and then waved his cap at the crew. He let out his best rebel yell and sent his horses after hers. The crowd shouted them off.

Up the street, many folks on the boardwalk waved and shouted to them. Several ran out of businesses to cheer on their departure. Slocum nodded and let the team trot up the sharp incline, behind hers.

"They sure appreciate us," Chris shouted, and he agreed.

When they finally reached the top of the pass, and with him chasing her dust, they swept across the sunny, flat valley for the rim. Reining up on the edge above the Verde Valley, they let their horses blow and settle down before they started the steep decline that clung to the canyon wall.

The sun was far in the west. He stood by the wagon and considered whether they should stay overnight at Thorpe's and make the mountains in the daylight.

"We'll spend the night down there," he said.

She raised her eyebrows, grinned, and nodded her approval. "Might save us going over the edge."

He agreed, watching a buzzard ride the updrafts. They would, without any trouble, make Fort Wingate round-trip in a week. He hunched his shoulders under the open coat. They were grateful for the warmth, as long shadows began to creep over them and the horses' shoes striking the rocks rang out across the yawning canyon. Spindly pines clung to the slopes above him. He held his horses down with the lines and watched ahead as she fought hers. Then he spit off the side and resumed his attention to the team. No room for error here.

The sun was far behind the mountain when they reached the valley floor and headed for Camp Verde. In the twilight, they passed a troop of black soldiers returning to the fort. Their blue uniforms trail-dusty, spent horses with heads down, still they smiled widely across their ebony faces and waved.

Slocum returned the salute and followed her to the crossing. The clear water was half-hub deep in the center of the ford. At the far side she let hers drink and Slocum waited for them to finish, letting his drop their heads on his side to fill their thirst.

When they had finished, she drove out and he followed. On the bank, she set them into a gallop and he brought up the rear. In front of Thorpe's, the man came out straightening his gallouses and nodding in approval.

"You two have got this business down," he said.

"How about a bed?" Slocum said, stepping down and handing the reins to the Mexican boy.

"We've got plenty," Thorpe said, bobbing his head.

"Good." Slocum turned to Chris and she nodded in approval.

"Come on in, she's got food ready," Thorpe said.

"I'll be back," Chris said and started around back.

"We'll be in there in a shake," Slocum said and followed her. He searched around recalling his incident with Doyle the last time, but he saw nothing out of place.

He waited outside the raw lumber privvy. She came out and held the door for him.

"Long in there and you might die," she teased.

"Sure don't smell like pie in here," he said and closed the door after himself.

"Where will he try us?" she asked outside as he emptied his bladder in the smelly hole cut out of the pine board.

"Who's that?" he asked, finishing his business and anxious to get out and breathe in the cleaner air.

"Dog Shit for one?"

"Hard to tell," he said, pushing his way out of the door and grateful for a fresh gasp of the air. "But somewhere up there he's got to try to stop us. That's the price he paid for them rifles and ammo by my way of thinking."

She shrugged. "We can't simply drive back to Fort Wingate, can we?"'

"No," he said, looked around to be certain they were alone, then he hugged her shoulder. He lowered his voice and spoke into her ear. "I sure hope he's got a private room for us."

She nodded and elbowed him. "So do I."

He straightened. "I'll make sure he's got one."

They washed up on the back porch. Thorpe came out the back door, using his suspenders for support.

"The mail's safe. Them horses will be harnessed at first light."

"One more thing," Slocum said. "You got us a room?"

Thorpe closed one eye and nodded somberly. "All fixed up for you and her."

"That's a secret," Slocum reminded him.

"It's with me."

"Good, come on, let's eat this man's great food." Slocum stood back for her to enter the lighted kitchen ahead of him.

"Any word of Doyle?" Slocum asked.

"None that I heard about."

"He'll turn up," Slocum said and went to the table to join her.

The meal was uneventful. Thorpe's wife served them plenty of spicy food, and they went off to the room he reserved for them. In the candle-lamp light, they undressed.

"Guess we better get some real sleep here. Be our last for a while, won't it?" she asked and caught his chin between her fingers. Her mouth raised to his, he quit struggling with his boots and kissed her. Their last night for several to share a bed, and he intended to savor it. His lips closed on hers and he smothered her in his arms.

At dawn, they struck out for the Mogollon rim. He took the lead and crossed the brown grass hills entering the mountains and pulling their horses down for the steeper grades. He planned to make Kay McNeal's by midnight that night. In the middle of the afternrnoon, they topped the rim and headed their weary horses for Denton's. Forced to slap them often to keep them running, he silently promised them grain, hay, and a good long rest for their efforts.

The sun high in the western sky, he swung his rig in the rancher's yard and the dogs heralded them. Chris was standing up to draw hers down when the rancher came on the run to greet them.

"Whew, you all are making good time," Denton said and took off his hat for her.

"Put that Stetson back on," she said and jumped down.

"Yes, ma'am."

"Dang you Isaac, I swear you about embarrass me."

"Not on purpose, but I sure am glad you two didn't have any mishaps or trouble this time."

"We're doing fine," Slocum said. "But we aim to make Kay's tonight."

"Be dark out there."

"Ain't no bears in the dark," she said, and they laughed.

"We'll catch them horses then," he said and took down a lariat from the corral. In a few minutes they were off for Kay's with Denton's shout of, "Good Luck!"

After sundown, Slocum tried to tell time by the North Star and Big Dipper. In his concern for the horses on the starlighted road and keeping them from veering off, he lost his concentration on keeping time. It was past midnight when they approached Kay's place.

When the dogs didn't begin bark, short of her place, he stood up and waved for Chris to come alongside him. They lacked a quarter-mile of the place. In the pearly light that shone on the bare cottonwoods, corrals, and buildings there were no lights. Over their hard-breathing horses, he turned his ear to listen for her herder dogs. None barked.

"What do you think?"

"Something's wrong, or her collies would be raising hell with us this close."

"What next? These horses are spent, they won't last for a run to the trading post."

"You stay here."

"No, where you go I go."

"Damnit—"

"I'm going along too."

Slocum was too busy thinking of his options to argue with her. "Here," he said, and handed her several sticks of fused blasting powder. "We may need them."

She put them in her coat pocket and took the scatter gun from the scabbard. He tied the teams together facing each other so they wouldn't panic or run off easily. Then with the Winchester in his hand, he waved for her to follow. He moved to the east to come in from the side, rather than the way one would expect them to show up.

At last from the security of the junipers, he tried to see what was happening. Glandings' horses were in the corral and stomping in their sleep. Good, they hadn't run off with them.

He told her to stay until he reached the back of the dark shed. If it looked safe he'd wave for her to join him. Bent over, he made a long run with the rifle in his right hand and reached the slab-sided shed.

Then, catching his breath, he eased himself to the corner. He blinked his eyes to be certain of what he saw. He spotted a white breechcloth. An armed Indian stood behind the corral. Damn. He wished for a stick of blasting powder. He'd loosen that buck's bowels.

Where was Kay? Then her voice shattered the night. "You no-account worthless piles of shit—you ain't shutting me up."

He held his finger up to silence Chris, who had joined him and was about to say, "That's Kay."

He took a stick of blasting powder from her, cut the fuse off short, and then cupped a match. He struck the flame to the twisting cord and the sparks began to sizzle. He tossed it over the shed, then clamped both hands over his ears and ducked down.

The blast blew two boards off the side of the shed and and made a billowing cloud of dust. Horses screamed in panic and several paints tore loose to run out of the yard. The Indian guard went to choking on the dust and started to run past them. Slocum struck him in the head with his rifle butt and the buck went down in a pile.

"Disarm him," he said to her, and cut off another fuse. He lit it and tossed it the other way over the shed. Both of them dropped, holding their ears. More horses shied away and the shouts of angry Indians in the confusion trying to contain their ponies drew a grin on Slocum's face. There were several leaving out. Good, less of them for him to fight with.

On his feet, he raced for the house, using various objects for cover and expecting to draw fire at any moment. Two Indians came charging out of the house, saw him, and ran to the side, yelping like he had hurt them.

He lit another and tossed it. When the blast went off, more charging paint horses came from that direction. Slocum barely made it to the porch to avoid being run over by the panicked animals. He wondered about Chris, who he left behind the shed.

"Come back you filthy sonsabitches!" Kay screamed.

"It's me, Slocum," he shouted and stepped inside to see that they had tied the woman to a chair.

Two shotgun blasts and he wondered what Chris was into. He drew out his big knife and cut Kay's binds. He gave the grateful woman his Colt and tore out the back door to check on Chris.

"Chris?" he shouted.

"I'm fine," she yelled back. "Just taking out the fighters."

"Get over here," he said and searched around in the dim light for any more.

"Them no-account scamps!" Kay said, coming out behind him. "I'll tack their tails to the shithouse door, I swear I will. Caught me unawares, but I kicked the hell out of them too."

"I imagine you did. We better get those tired horses changed. How many were there?" he asked.

"Maybe ten, I couldn't count them."

"There's damn sure less now."

"I ever get my hands on that stinking Navajo, I'll whack him off between the legs and he'll squat to pee."

"That the last of them?" Chris asked, searching around.

Slocum shook his head. "Maybe over for now, but they ain't through yet."

"They ain't stopped us, you mean?" Chris asked and Slocum nodded in agreement, lighting a lamp.

"Lord, I was so afraid you'd drive in and they'd jump you," Kay said.

"We would have, but the dogs weren't barking."

"Yeah, them no accounts killed them earlier. You two must be done in."

"We're all right. We slept at Denton's," he said from the doorway, standing on his toes to try and see beyond the corral.

"Well, bless my stars. You've sure got some grit in your craw, girl."

"Some," Chris said and laughed. "Some."

They switched harnesses. The renegades had raided her kitchen, but Kay managed to find some sourdough bread and ham for them to eat. With the fresh animals hitched, they ate their food.

"They may come back," Slocum said. "You might ought to come to the trading post with us."

"They jumped me once. I won't let them have that chance again."

"You may not have a chance," Slocum said, concerned for her safety.

"No blanket-assed bucks are running me off."

He could see no amount of arguing would change her mind. He drew a deep breath, then washed down his food with a dipper of water. Thank heavens; the deepest cold might have let up. Better get on their way.

He clapped Kay on the shoulders, told her to be on guard, and nodded to Chris. She climbed on her buckboard, undid the reins, and in minutes they were headed east under the star-flecked sky along the Little Colorado's course.

Dawn winked in the purple east. In the frosty air, they exhaled great clouds of vapors, stomped their cold feet while the hard-breathing horses rested.

"What about Kay?" she asked.

Slocum glanced back. He still felt concerned about leaving her, but short of tying her up, she would never have consented to leaving her place.

He shook his head. "I hated she wouldn't come along."

"You think Dog Shit will go back there?"

"She's probably the most vulnerable post."

Chris agreed without another word, but he could see her unspoken concern. Then it was drive on, they reached the trading post by midmorning.

Pasquel came hurrying out. "*Madres Dios*, you are driving *muya* hard, *mis amigos*."

"Got to get the mail through," Slocum said, tying off his reins and climbing down.

"Sleep?" the big man asked.

Slocum considered the notion, then he looked at the way Chris came across the yard with her eyes half open. She was done in. Might even cave in, if he didn't stop for some rest.

"A few hours," he said, and she smiled with a nod of appreciation.

Slocum woke up duller than he went to sleep. After two cups of coffee, he felt awake enough to eat the platter of food in front of him. Chris swept her hair back and smiled at him from across the table.

"Short nap," she said.

He agreed.

"I know—bath, bed and sleep . . ."

"Another twenty-four hours."

"Will the horses be there? Near Maggard's, I mean. We'll get there early at this rate."

"They better be."

She shrugged and picked at her food.

"You all right?" he asked, looking around the post. Seeing nothing out of place, he turned back to her.

"Why do I have this bad feeling?"

"I don't know. What about?"

"About you."

"You a witch?" he asked with a grin.

"No, but I sure have something grating on my brain."

"You better eat up, we need to make tracks."

"If anything happens to you . . ."

"You deliver the mail, that's what you do. Now eat your food, you'll need the strength."

She shook her head as if still deeply engrossed in her concern. Then she began to eat her breakfast. He excused himself and went to find the buckboards. There were a few things he still needed to do. In the warming sun, he armed the last six blasting sticks.

Pasquel came out and joined him. Slocum related the problems at Kay's and the renegades.

"Someone should kill that worthless Dog Shit. I need to put a bounty on his head."

"I'll get Glanding to put up some money for that," Slocum offered, putting his loaded sticks in the box. "Hell, no telling how much he cost him already."

Pasquel nodded in deep consideration. "Yes, I will talk to my boss. He robs our customers after they leave here. Takes their food and supplies they trade for."

"I'll speak to Glanding about it when I get there."

"Drive safely, *amigo*."

"We will. Thanks," Slocum said and saw her hurrying across the yard. "We better make tracks."

She climbed on her rig and he mounted his seat. With a nod, they were headed for Fort Wingate. Slocum saw Pasquel waving in their dust. The final leg, if there were fresh horses at the line, and they would be at Fort Wingate by midnight. Under the seven days. He threw the lines to his horses. They had lots of ground to cover in the next hours of light left in the day. She led the way, and wasn't wasting any of it either.

Slocum wondered what had her so concerned. Intuition could be a life-saver and women had a lot more of it than men. He would need to keep his wits about him. For the moment, he savored more the notion of a bath, a warm bed, and her silky-skinned body curled up inside his arms.

18

Glanding's men had their fresh horses ahead. Under the stars, they reached the road to Maggard's and awoke the three armed Mexicans with their arrival.

"Señor Slocum?" one called out.

"*Si*" he shouted, and drew in his hard-breathing team.

"Any problems?" the man asked.

"No, you have any?"

The man shook his head and set his rifle aside. "But we wondered if you were coming."

"Been here long?" Slocum asked.

"We came before sundown, so we could find a place."

"Anything happening in Wingate?"

The man shrugged as if it was business as usual.

"Good," Slocum said, latching harness buckles. "We should be there by midnight or a little past."

"He is going to make a new station near here," the man said.

"Needs one. Did they kill Pearcy?"

"*Si*. Senor Maggard looks for the ones who did it. He came by and spoke to us last night."

"He needs to ride west. They raided Kay's before we got there."

The man nodded as they finished the harness change. Slocum threaded the reins back.

"Chris, you about ready?"

"Ready," she said, and he could see her outline standing on the buckboard.

"Let's head for Wingate."

"Great. I need a bath and a bed."

"So do I. Go!"

"*Gracias*," he said over his shoulders and set the team after hers.

They arrived at two A.M., awoke Glanding who, sleepy-eyed and husky-voiced, came out of his office and clapped Slocum on the shoulder.

"You done it. When can you go back?"

"In a day. Those renegades hit Kay's place. She was all right, but I'm not certain they didn't go back after we left."

Glanding cleared his throat and spat out a big hocker on the ground. "I told that damn Colonel up there at the fort about that Dog Shit Injun."

Slocum had no time to explain to the man about the lack of army scout personnel. "The folks at the trading post want to issue a reward for his head."

"Count me in."

Slocum acknowledged his reply and looked over at Chris, who lounged at the near rig. She was done in. "I need a bath and some sleep. How much mail you have piled up here?"

"What do you mean?" Glanding asked.

"One or two rigs?"

"Two, hell, I must have all the Christmas mail there is."

"We can take two," he said and tossed his head to her. They were leaving, he had better things to do than to stand around in the cold night air and talk to Glanding.

"I'll have them ready," Glanding shouted after him.

With Chris under his arm, Slocum waved that he heard the man. God sake, for now he wanted to forget it all. He wanted the wagon wheels to stop churning in his head, wanted the drum of the horses' hooves to grow silent, and he wanted more than anything else to savor her lithe body beneath him in a clean bed.

19

The sunlight spilled in the grimy window onto the floor. Diffused by the film of dirt on the glass, it still warmed the air in the room. He laid back with his hands cupped under his head and studied the tin ceiling tiles. She was still asleep, her shapely warm butt against his side, her quiet breathing sounding like a low hum.

Somehow someone needed to stop the renegade Dog Shit. No way that Slocum could do it, driving the buckboard on that tight a schedule. The army was worthless. They sent out patrols that couldn't find an old toothless squaw. Made long rides in big circles and learned nothing. The scout system was what worked and they obviously had none worth a pinch of salt. He drew in a deep breath and exhaled.

Where had Doyle gone? That worthless piece of cow dung could still be in the picture. If someone had hired him to stop the mail runs, then they must be getting antsy with the mail finally getting through.

Slocum was struck with a picture of the one-eyed redhead Humphrey rushing out the back door of the bunkhouse. Him on his belly in the bunk trying to get down in time to stop him, and Banks too late at the back door. Nice bunch of characters to have on the loose. A rapist he owed, a killer Chris wanted brought to justice, and a band of renegades who needed to be rounded up or shot.

He closed his eyes—and another hurried trip to Prescott loomed in the offing. How long could he do this? Make these runs? An article in that *Daily Miner* in Prescott might filter down to the wrong folks, and then the Abbott Brothers could be waiting for him when he drove in on either end. If he didn't have her luscious naked body in the bed with him, he would have been damn depressed by it all.

They spent the day in bed making love. Except for trips to eat at Rosa's, they lounged on the mattress, soaking up all the ecstasy of two uninhibited bodies searching and exploring and probing. Even when he knew there was no more, she gently coaxed another blinding orgasm from him.

"When must you go?" she finally asked, sprawled on his chest.

"Like leave these parts?"

"Yes."

He shook his head. "I never know. I hope a day before they show up."

"But they will come for you, won't they?"

"Yes. What will you do when I'm gone?"

"Drive the mail run, if Glanding will let me."

"Ain't much of a job for—"

She laid her fingers over his lips. "I could get a job in that big cat house in Preskitt."

"How do you know about it?" he frowned at her.

"I was headed there to work when I met you."

"Oh."

"There ain't much a wanton woman can do to make a living."

He nodded. "Before I leave, I'll convince Glanding to keep you on."

"Good," she said, satisfied, and twisted the hairs on his chest in her fingertips.

A hard knock on the door and he scrambled for his

Colt. With it in his hand, he frowned at her and answered, "Who's there?"

"Maggard. Need to talk to you. They say you seen that renegade Dog Shit."

Slocum threw the covers off his legs and shook his head. "Let me get dressed."

"Take your time."

He shrugged at her and she agreed. In moments, she was wiggling her way into her pants. He dressed slowly to give her enough time. This was the man who had beaten up the renegade for messing with his traps. The late Pearcy's boss.

Satisfied she was decent, Slocum nodded to her and went across the room to open the door.

"Didn't mean to bust up your sleep, but I rode a horse to death getting here—" A bear of a man over six feet tall with a bushy black beard stood in the hallway resting a Sharp's buffalo gun on the floor beside him.

"Slocum." He stuck out a hand and wondered if he'd draw back a stub.

"Proud to meetcha. Howdy," he said, coming in the room after Slocum.

"Christine, this is Maggard."

The big man ripped off his floppy-brimmed hat and his eyes about bugged out at the sight of her. "Christine? Why I'm proud to meetcha."

He held out a great paw and shook her hand as dainty as if it were a butterfly. She nodded and then stepped back.

"She's dressed like that because she's the other mail driver," Slocum said.

"Oh, yes. Dangerous work for such a pretty woman."

"I'm hoping to end that dangerous part," Slocum said.

"I want to help. You told them Mexicans that Dog Shit was harrassing one of the other relay stations."

"I gave them a good dusting with blasting powder out at Kay McNeal's where the road turns south for the Little Colorado. But I'm concerned they'll be back."

"Could I ride with you two out there? Then, if I find them I'll go after them."

"Have to ask Glanding."

"Oh, he's the one sent me over here to ask you two."

"Fine, you be at the office at sunup, but we don't waste much time," Slocum said. The man needed to be warned. They had to move to make the schedule and they weren't waiting on him.

"Won't bother me what time you want to go. I want that renegade run down. Pearcy was a longtime friend of mine and they killed him. I want them to pay." He bowed for Chris and then with a smile that showed his lips and teeth under the thick mat of beard and mustache, he said, "You're a lucky man, Slocum, to have the likes of her to share your business."

Slocum agreed and showed him to the door. When he closed it he looked at her and they both smiled.

"Big man," he said.

"Big as a grizzly," she said and hugged him.

" 'Cept he's on our side," he said, rocking her back and forth in his arms.

Dawn was still a small seam of blue flannel when Slocum checked over the harness by lantern light. Glanding held up the light for him.

"Looks all right?" the big man asked.

"Yes." Slocum looked around to be certain that they were alone. "If I have to leave, I want you to hire her to drive in my place."

"Without you—"

"Damnit, Glanding, listen. She needs work, not a hard time. Let her drive, should I have to leave."

"All right, but how could a whip of a girl—"

"She can do it."

"She'll drive then."

"Good, that's settled."

"Where in hell are you going?"

"Crazy," he said and saw her coming out of the office with their large passenger guard, Maggard.

"Be careful, and consider I'm paying you good wages before you run off," Glanding said, under his breath. "I need both of you."

"Keep an eye out for Doyle, and you see if you can learn who wants this mail contract."

"I will, and I've got friends in Sante Fe listening too," Glanding said.

"Good," Slocum said and turned to Maggard and Chris. "You two can ride double. Chris, you take the lead."

"You have got horses back out there?" Slocum asked Glanding.

"Oh, yes, and we're going to build a new station too."

After an exchange of pleasantries, Maggard nodded to him and went over to climb on the seat beside Chris. Slocum figured the bench seat was too small for the two of them. He noted the big man carried the Sharp's and guessed he could use it. Somehow Maggard was a lot younger than he had imagined he would be, but still a bear of man and no doubt iron-wood tough. He was maybe only in his thirties, and Slocum had originally expected someone twice that age.

They reached the line by midday and swapped horses. There had been no sign of renegades according to Glanding's Mexicans, who acted less nervous this time than before.

"Don't take chances," Slocum warned them. "Those red devils are still out here."

They agreed they wouldn't, and in the shake of a lamb's tail they were headed west. Slocum felt a little twinge of jealousy. Maggard and Chris had struck up a conversation and when they drew up for a breather stop, they were both laughing and preoccupied.

When she returned from relieving herself, she crossed over to where Slocum sat on his haunches.

"We'll be to the trading post by midnight?"

"Yes, and sleep a few hours there."

"Do you think they raided Kay's again?"

"I hope not."

"So do I," she said and looked off to the distant mountains in the south.

"Glanding said he would employ you when I had to leave."

"Oh, thanks." And she smiled warmly at him.

"You ready, Maggard?" he shouted to the man.

"Ready." He waved his long rifle and climbed onto the other buckboard. Chris hurried to join him.

They reached Markam's trading post close to midnight. Pasquel came out with a lamp.

"Ho, it is you, Señor Maggard with these crazy drivers."

"They'd wear a fellow's fanny off," the big man said, climbing down.

"We get four hours sleep here," Slocum informed him. "Grab your bedroll."

"She'll get you rooms," Pasquel said and waved them toward the front door.

"Almost too quiet, ain't it?" Chris asked, walking beside him.

"Almost," Slocum agreed, looking around the dark yard. No sign all day of the renegades or anyone else beside the usual road traffic of freighters, folks moving west, and peaceful Indians.

They were up and eating breakfast before dawn. The chill of the night had invaded the post's interior. Chris shivered underneath her poncho, busy eating her food.

"Going to be colder than all get-out today," Maggard said between bites. Chris quickly agreed.

"At least you've got him to block the wind," Slocum teased her.

"I could use a wood stove," she said and went back to cutting her food.

They headed west and made Kay's by midafternoon. She came out carrying a rifle and pushing a strand of loose hair back.

"No renegades?" Slocum asked, jumping down, relieved to see her safe.

She shook her head and grinned in recognition at Maggard. "Where've you been?" she asked.

"Aw, looking for gold, doing some trapping," the big man began, and Slocum went for the fresh horses. At this rate, they could make it to Denton's by midnight. They needed to hurry. He called to Chris.

"Coming," Chris said and fell in on his heels.

The three were off in ten minutes, taking leave of Kay's and on the road that swung south. It was past midnight when they drew up under the stars in Denton's yard. Slocum was half asleep and dropped heavily to the ground.

Strange, Slocum thought. Denton usually rushed out and . . . Slocum dismissed it, dragged out his bedroll. There was a light in the cabin, he must be getting dressed. Chris had hers and so did Maggard.

Tired to the bone, but feeling good about the distance they'd made, Slocum's eyes suddenly flew open at the sight of the one-eyed Humphrey in the doorway holding a gun on him.

"You sumbitches, get your hands up and get in here!"

"How in the hell . . ." Slocum felt like he'd been kicked in the crotch. Inside and seated at the table was the grinning Doyle.

"Well, Slocum, this time I have the upper hand," Doyle announced confidently, drumming his fingers on the tabletop.

"Who in the hell are you?" Maggard demanded.

"Who's asking?" Doyle said, rising from the chair, while Humphrey disarmed them.

"Maggard's my name."

"Take a seat," Doyle said and gave the big man a shove with his hand.

Slocum saw the rage in Maggard's eyes. It might be the only chance they had. He swung both hands and slammed Humphrey against the wall. Chris dove for the gun that went flying and Maggard's roar shook the china tea cups in the cabinet.

Slocum leaped on top of Humphrey, driving his fist into the man like a piston on a steam engine. From the corner of his eye he saw Doyle fly through the air and then slide down the log wall to his butt. The one-eyed killer looked through fighting when Slocum gathered up a fistful of his shirt and shoved him back down to cower on the floor.

Chris broke a chair over Doyle's head to finish him off. He lay unconscious on the floor. Maggard came across the floor like a rampaging bruin, jerked Humphrey to his feet, and drove a massive fist into the man's face. The killer went limp as a dishrag.

"Whew!" Chris said, looking around the room. "Kinda cleaned up on some unwanted guests. Where's Isaac?"

Slocum spotted the rancher's boots turned toes-up, and stuck out his arm to stop her. "Don't go back there," he said and went to drop to haunches beside the still body. The blood on the man's shirt told him enough. He closed the blank eyes, then closed his own. They'd killed him.

"He's dead?" Maggard asked from behind him.

"Oh, no," she cried. "Isaac was a good—"

Slocum rose to his feet and hugged her. "He sure thought lots of you."

"The world don't need the likes of them two. The law can't stop them. We need to," Maggard said.

Slocum agreed numbly. What did they do to bandits in Mexico? Stand them against an adobe wall and use a firing squad. Cut off their heads with a sword in Turkey. Used a guillotine in France, and at one time even tore them apart with horses pulling them in four directions. He had once read about hungry men hung in England for stealing bread—was this justice?

"You mean to hang them?" Slocum asked, breaking his thoughts.

"Yes."

"Let's get on with it," Slocum said and grasped the limp Doyle by the collar. "Sooner we send these two to hell the better place this world will be."

"What about Isaac?" Chris asked, trailing after them as each one took a prisoner outside.

"We'll wrap him up. Cold as it is, he'll be fine in the

house and we'll send a party back to give him a decent burial."

She looked back at the house in the starlight, then hurried to keep up with them.

"Who hired you?" Slocum asked Doyle.

"You'll never know," the outlaw grumbled.

"For a man about to tread air, you better get to thinking up names," Maggard said, dragging the moaning Humphrey up to stand with his associate.

Slocum went and found their saddle horses and brought them up. Then he located a couple of Isaac's ropes. He heard a scuffle and reached for his Colt, but it looked like Maggard had things under control. He brought the ponies up close.

"It was Ed Martin." Doyle spit out a tooth and the dark blood on his chin showed in the pearly light.

"Martin wanted the mail contract?" Slocum asked as he bound Humphrey's hands behind his back.

"Yeah."

"He hire the renegades too?"

"I don't know . . ."

"You need a memory recovery?" Maggard demanded.

"I swear—Ed Martin of Sante Fe hired me! That's all I know."

"I know enough," Slocum said, feeling weighted by the information, and throwing the first rope over the crossarm. "You two got any words for your salvation?"

"Go to hell," Humphrey said. "And same to that bitch over there."

Slocum put the noose on his neck and smiled grimly at the killer. "I'll sure be looking forward to seeing you there. Hold the door open."

"Get up there," Maggard said and shoved Humphrey on his horse. Slocum tied the rope off so there was little slack.

A noose was fashioned on Doyle's throat and Maggard tossed him in the saddle. Slocum made sure the rope was secure. He walked over to join Maggard and they busted both horses in the butt at the same time. The ponies bolted away, the ropes screeched, and the two killers danced under the stars. Then, without looking at the pair, they headed for the cabin. Slocum herded Chris under his arm.

She wept. He and Maggard wrapped up Denton's corpse, stowed it in the back room where it would be cold enough. Then they lay down to sleep, but Slocum's eyes would not close. He wanted to comfort the upset Chris, but even holding her in his arms didn't help.

At dawn, she made coffee and stirred up some fried potatoes from Denton's cupboard to feed them. Red-eyed, she poured them coffee in the lamplight.

"He deserved better," she said and paused.

"Damn sure did," Slocum agreed, picking up his cup. He blew the steam off the surface and studied the small window. Sometimes life had twists that seemed unfair. A picture of the two killers hanging limp with their heads to the side was imprinted in his mind from the trip outside to relieve his bladder.

Some wolf pups needed to be hit in the head at birth.

20

"Isaac Denton's dead?" Thorpe asked in disbelief.

"Yes," Slocum said, dropping heavily from the buck-board. "Need a burying party to go up there. We left him wrapped up in the back room, figured he'd keep as cold as it was."

"Sure. I'll get some folks to help me and head up there. But who—"

"They're up there too. You'll have to cut them down."

"Good enough, come on inside, she's got food ready. Guess you need fresh horses?"

"Yes. This is Maggard." He introduced the big man.

Pleasantries exchanged, they went inside the building. Chris still acting numb over Denton's death, Slocum tried to comfort her.

"Warmer down here," he said guiding her inside.

"But we get over that rim up there, it will be cold again," she reminded him and forced a smile.

"Yeah, but you know what?"

"A hot bath and a bed?"

"You bet."

"I'll be ready for it."

"Excuse the kids," Thorpe apologized to them as four

173

youngsters wrapped strings of popcorn on a juniper tree set up in the big room.

"Hey, they won't bother us," Maggard said.

"No," Slocum said, wondering what day it was.

"It'll be Christmas in two days and they wanted to put up a tree," Thorpe said. "You kids hold it down over there."

"Aw, no," Maggard said. "That's the best thing I've seen or heard in years."

Slocum agreed. Then he turned and saw the smile on Chris's lips and the rainbows in the beads of tears on her cheeks. The children acted uninhibited, as the older sister pointed to the boy on the chair how he needed to loop the chain higher.

In half an hour, they were back on the road, headed for the pass above Camp Verde and their destination, Preskitt. They rested at the summit and then raced across the long valley, finally pulling the last grade until the lights of the capitol shown like twinkling stars.

Slocum felt some of the tension leave his body hurrying down the western slope toward their destination. They might make the whole run in six days this time. That would shock old Glanding.

He pulled up at the livery. He saw Chris run off to use the facilities out back. Reins tied off, he stretched his arms over his head and yawned. Then she came out of the alleyway on the run.

"Come with me," she hissed, looking around as Maggard talked to the livery boy.

"What's wrong?" he asked as she hurried him inside.

The wine smell of horse piss and manure filled his nose. Then he saw in the tie stall what she had discovered. The Apaloosa horse, his great blanket of black moons obvious in the small light coming from the office window.

"Is it his?" she asked breathlessly.

Slocum looked over his shoulder and turned back with a sharp nod to her. Damn! The Abbott Brothers were in Preskitt looking for him. Probably over on Whiskey Row at that very minute asking a million questions and getting some answers.

"What are you going to do?"

"Nothing else I can do."

"Oh, no!" She tackled him and buried her face in his poncho.

"You and Maggard can take back the mail. Glanding owes me for a run-and-a-half. You collect it with yours."

"What will you do?"

"Catch a horse and ride on."

"What about the one in Fort Wingate?"

"Sell him and keep the money."

"I'll buy you a horse," she protested.

"No."

"Damnit," she swore, "I'm buying one. Let's go talk to the boy about one." Then she paused. "Can we trust Maggard?"

"I think so, he ain't got no allegiance to them two."

"I'll tell him while you get the horse and saddle you need." She looked around, then savagely kicked a pile of horse apples down the alleyway. "Damnit to hell, Slocum—I know you said—but, I wasn't ready to give you up."

"Me owing you a bath and bed, you mean."

"Ah, that's not it. Yes, it is. We better get you a horse and rig. I'll handle Maggard."

"You can," he said and smiled in the dim light of the stables.

In ten minutes, aboard a short coupled mustang, he left out the back way of the stables, while Chris and Maggard stayed out front to answer any questions and hold off the Abbott brothers from finding him when the pair learned the Fort Wingate mail had arrived. How would they know that two of them hadn't brought in the buckboards? Before the drunks all poured out of the bars to see about their postal things, Slocum had gone over the pass and headed across the valley.

He slept a few hours before dawn in his bedroll, then rode off into the Verde Valley. He skirted Thorpe's and the settlement, places that he might be regconized and reported to the bounty hunters, in the event they rode his back trail.

Long past dark, he reached Denton's place. The outlaws had been cut down and the three fresh mounds told him the job had been done. No sign of anyone, he built a fire in the stove to drive some of the cold out of his bones. He made some coffee and cooked some potaotes from the cellar with some bacon he found in the there too.

The wind howled at the eaves and he ate the food, disappointed in the taste. He graphically recalled the rape, and the room held little comfort for him, despite the warming of the fire in the stove. Poor Isaac Denton, shot down so some greedy bastard could steal the mail contract. And Chris—thoughts of her lithe body brought a knot to his throat.

He could imagine capturing one of her small breasts in his hand and making her pointed nipple turn rock hard. Running his palm over the silky skin of her flat belly until at last he cupped her pubic mound and eased his finger down the seam. Her soft moans of pleasure escaping the soft lips sweet as honeycomb. Damn. He closed his eyes to his loss.

Before dawn he rode north. Midafternoon, he reached Kay's and saw the front door open. His hand slid to the Colt grips as he looked about for any sign and held down the mustang. No horses in the pens.

Damn, those renegades had struck again. He sharply checked the bay and dismounted, tying him to juniper. Every muscle in his body tensed, he swiveled his head around at any sound. In a hurry to see what he could learn, still he used caution for fear that some of them might still be there.

He wasn't ready for the sight of her bloody naked body on the floor. His eyes closed, his shoulder sagged against the doorway. The renegades had no doubt raped her, then tortured her.

He swallowed back the urge to puke. The sourness riding the back of his tongue, he searched the ransacked cabin for a blanket. At last he found a Navajo rug and rolled her hardly recognizable stiff body in it. Then he roped it tight around her form, all the time thinking that he wanted her buried before Chris returned and found her like that.

Fighting involuntary tears that ran down his cheek, he went to find a shovel. In a few hours, he finished the grave and buried her with a small silent prayer, covered her up, and staggered back to the house. Unable to stand the sight of the blood stains on the floor, he went to his bay.

After feeding him some of her sweet hay, he took down his bedroll and slept for a few hours. He was unsure what he could do about horses for her and Maggard. Then, waking in the darkness, he had an idea of how to help them. Ride to the trading post and have Pasquel meet them halfway or so with fresh ones.

He loaded the bedroll and drew up the cinch. Searching around in the starlight, he gave a great exhale, dreading the ride on the short coupled pony with his stiff gait.

"Old pony, we're making a fast, cold ride tonight," he said and swung up. He reined him around the shed and headed east in a long lope. They had miles to make.

He reached the trading post in the middle of the night and had them awaken Pasquel.

"They killed Kay and stole the horses. I need you to take some fresh horses and meet Chris & Maggard part of the way."

"Dog Shit do it?" Pasquel said.

"I think so. It wasn't a pretty sight."

"Him and her coming?"

"Yes," Slocum said. "But they'll need fresh horses."

"You get something to eat and we'll talk," Pasquel said, the sleep still in his voice. He hurried off, and the smiling Mexican woman put on her apron.

"*Uno momento,*" she said and hurried off to the kitchen in back.

Slocum took a seat at a table in the empty trading post. Where was Dog Shit at?

Pasquel slid in a chair across from him. "I learned they

have a camp at a spring north of here. When the sun rises we will ride up there and end this one's life."

"He's well-armed."

"Hmm," Pasquel snuffed. "He is stupid too. He robbed several Navajos of their supplies they traded for. They won't protect him. He kidnapped a young girl too. Rifles won't protect him."

Slocum shrugged and then nodded. "I'll be ready to ride when you are."

"I have a fresh horse for you."

The woman brought some lukewarm coffee and apologized that the food would be a while, for her fire had gone out.

"No problem." Slocum smiled at her. "I know it will be good when you bring it."

They rode out in the cold dawn with a boy called Juan, who Pasquel said could track a mouse on rocks. Headed north, Slocum rode a long-bodied sorrel that had a smooth-swinging trot. They went through the yellow chalky-colored land following twisted wagon tracks.

A Navajo man wrapped in a colorful blanket rode up and spoke to Pasquel in his native tongue, then nodded and fell in with them.

Pasquel dropped back and put his horse beside Slocum's.

"That is Henry Johns. It was his niece they kidnapped."

Slocum acknowledged it.

In the next hour a dozen more Navajos, one at a time, joined them. Silent and solemn-faced, they rode in to become part of the posse. Slocum could see they all carried rifles under their blankets. Riding paint horses, they pushed north toward the range of stratified layers of rock showing colors of red, purple, and tans.

Few words passed as the posse trotted their horses, stirring up gusts of dust that swirled around their horses' legs. A cold sun shone brightly on them. The boy Juan came riding back on his sweating horse.

"They are at the spring," he said when they reined up to face him.

Pasquel nodded and spoke to them. Slocum saw him make the sign of a circle with his hand, giving each man a spoke of the wheel with a point at each individual, who agreed with a nod.

"We will wait here," Pasquel said, "until they are in place."

Slocum agreed and undid his cinch.

The two men squatted under the lip of the rise, absorbing all the solar source they could.

"This is serious business. These men have had enough of Dog Shit. I am letting them handle it in their way."

Slocum agreed. Then he recalled some small cigars in his pocket and shared one with the man. He lit his and Pasquel's off a match, and both sat back on their haunches to wait and smoke.

Slowlike he exhaled the smoke. How was Chris making it? He hoped her and Maggard made it all right. Damn, he wished he was there—his thoughts were shattered by the clatter of rifle fire.

He glanced over at Pasquel. Should they go help?

"They need help, they're to send Juan for us."

Slocum went to his haunches again and drew on the cigar. He let the hot smoke fill his mouth and inhaled it. The nicotine spread in his bloodstream and settled some of his restlessness. More shots. Then only the cry of ravens.

In a short while all the men returned. Their stoic faces revealed nothing. The young girl bare-headed and wrapped in a bright red-and-black pattern blanket rode a pony and followed them. New rifles stuck out of panniers on board a mule.

The first rider nodded. "Sumbitch no more." With that, they booted their horses on, and the procession rode by with each man nodding to them and going on.

Pasquel finished his cigar and ground out the butt. "Shame they didn't do that a long time ago."

Slocum agreed and went for his horse. He looked off at the azure sky and pushed up the fender skirt. *Sorry,*

Kay, we were too late to save you. He drew up the cinch and nodded to Pasquel.

"That rounds that up."

"You aren't driving?"

"It's a long story. No, I'm through driving."

"Glanding will miss you." Pasquel frowned as the boy Juan joined them.

"Chris can do it. Dog Shit and the others are gone now." He wanted to add, except one, Ed Martin.

They swung up and Pasquel spoke to the boy. "All of them gone?"

"See the smoke," the boy pointed.

Slocum turned and glimpsed at a tall column streaking the horizon. They no doubt had burned Dog Shit and his gang's bodies in a log hogan. That part was over. He put the sorrel in a long trot for the post.

21

Slocum drew rein on the bay gelding. He had circled around to enter Sante Fe from the north. A sharp wind tried to tear away the blanket poncho as he booted the pony downhill. His presence here didn't need to be known. He wanted Ed Martin to pay for what he'd had done to Kay and Denton and Chris. The man's greed for money was all it was over. For Martin to hire no-accounts like Doyle was bad enough, but for him to arm those Navajo renegades so they could prey on the other peaceful Indians as well as the mail run was worse.

He'd find him. And for Kay and the others he'd even the score. He reined the horse off onto a pathway. The junipers crowded the way and the pungent-smelling boughs brushed his legs and shoulders. At last he spotted the small shed and corrals. He wondered if she would be home at midday.

He put the horse in the pen, lossened the cinch, but did not unsaddle him. Uncertain about the Abbott brothers' whereabouts, he moved to the front door of the small adobe house and knocked. No answer.

He squatted down in the weak sunshine and tried to stay warm. She should be returning, for it was late afternoon. He decided it would be warmer for him to split wood. So he went to the wood pile and began to use the well-worn ax. The sticks busted in two by his overhead swings, the amount of ready wood began to grow.

At last, he saw her running up the path from the road below, a great smile on her face. Either he must be welcome, or else she needed her wood split. Nana was short, but her lithe body under the dress and blanket still shapely. Her black hair was tied in a scarf against the cold, and she rushed up and hugged his midsection.

"You came back?" she said out of breath.

He looked off to the east at the snow caps. How could he tell her he would only be there for a short time? But he must.

Deliberately, he raised her chin with the side of his hands and looked into her pleading brown eyes. Her soft, pouty lower lip tucked under the top one in expectation of his words.

"I can't stay long."

"You are here though. Why are you outside? Do you have a fire built?"

"I was not going in until you returned."

"It is your *casa* too."

He stopped and loaded his arms with wood. "I was working."

"So I see, and you have split much wood." She paused to open the door and looked back at him. "How will I ever repay you?"

"I can think of ways," he said, then smiled at her.

"Good," she said and opened the door for him.

"Are you hungry?" she asked as he rebuilt the fire in the hearth.

"For what?"

"My bed or food?" She stood with her hands on her slender hips.

"Not food," he said, feeling grateful for the room's warmth, and with the fire restored, he knew it would soon be much warmer.

She smiled coyly at him when he rose from his work

and she began to undo her skirt. "Get undressed, big man."

"I like decisive women."

She wrinkled her small nose at him. "You like women, Slocum."

Toeing off his boots, he had to agree. The notion of the pleasure ahead for him made his head swirl. He almost forgot his purpose in coming to Sante Fe.

"You know an Ed Martin lives here?"

She raised up with her blouse half off and then shook her head.

"Never mind," he said, a little short of breath at the prospect of taking on the slinky body before him. "It ain't a damn bit important who he is right now."

Later that night in town, Slocum learned from a barmaid in the Los Hombres Bar that Ed Martin lived in an adobe a few blocks up Frio Wash. In the darkness of night, he moved with care up the sandy road, that in times of rain funnelled the runoff into these larger fingers of gulches to feed the Rio Grande.

The moonlight showed on the snowy mountains high above him. He at last found the house the girl had told him about. With his collar turned up, he studied the lights in the windows.

There was a party inside. He could hear the fiddle strings and the shouts of the fun seekers. How long would they stay? He hunched his shoulders against the night cold and waited.

Past midnight, they continued. A few left by buggy and horse, but the rest kept up their revelry inside the house. At long last, weary of waiting, Slocum headed down the road.

He reached Nana's small shack and first checked on the bay stabled in her small shed. Then he rapped on the door. Waiting in the cold, he searched about. He turned back in time for her to crack it open.

"Why didn't you come inside?" she asked in a dry, sleepy voice. She yawned and stretched her hand over her head. Dressed in a longtailed white shift that shone in the moonlight flooding in the small windows, she closed the door and bolted it.

"I was afraid you might have company," he teased, grateful to be inside and out of the chill.

"Ha, with you in Santa Fe. You find that Martin somebody?"

"Yes, but there was party at his *casa*."

"It will be Christmas soon, they are celebrating. You coming to bed with me?" she asked and bent way over in the flickering orange of the fire.

"Why?" A smile creased in the corners of his mouth

"Well," she said, still bent over. "I was going to take off this long nightgown if you are."

"Take it off." He smiled and toed off his boots.

"Good," she said and pulled the garment off over her head. "You don't be long. It is cold in here without my clothes." She wrapped her arms around her naked form in the pearly light coming in the small window and went to stand beside the bed.

"I'm hurrying fast as I can."

"Not fast enough," she complained and lay on the mattress holding the covers back for him.

"Boy, you've got bossy since the last time."

"Too long without you makes me like that."

He slid in the bed and she tossed the covers over him. Then after fussing about them, she squirmed down until she was on her side facing him.

"What do you want for Christmas?" he asked in her ear.

Her small hand shot downward and closed on his half erection. "This."

"This is your early Merry Christmas," he whispered in her ear as she scooted underneath him.

In minutes, she had him hard and inside her, his hips pumping against hers. He raised himself up on his hands to savor his efforts in and out of her. Her back arched, her belly shoved at him, and soft cries of unrestrained pleasure escaped her lips.

His world tilted and spun off into a giddiness that left him weightless too. Her contractions closed on his stinging wand and he fought harder and harder for relief. At last, he exploded into the darkness of her palace of pleasure. They fell in a heap and slept.

In the frosty morning, he fed the bay horse a good bait of corn and some old hay on hand. Hatless, he moved about the streets of Sante Fe under a blanket like so many of the Indians and natives, who tried to ward off the cold.

He eased inside the Elephant Bar, careful that no dealers recognized him. In the corner, he drank a quick jigger of good whiskey. From the barmaid's description of the man the night before, Martin was not in there. Slocum left and pushed down the street, to next try the Double Eagle. No Martin. He guessed the man was sleeping off his hangover from the party.

In his blanket coat, Slocum traipsed up and down the streets, jubilant children raced about shouting. People on the sidewalks smiled at him with the benevolence shown to poor men on holidays and he nodded, pleased that his disguise worked. Then he caught sight of his quarry.

Dressed in a suit with a black coat open for the midday sun's growing warmth, Martin crossed the street and went inside a cafe across the square. Slocum stood with his back to the adobe wall. Then he went close to the cafe, dropped on his butt, and pressed his back to the wall.

Martin emerged and spoke to another man dressed in a suit.

"Hey, Martin, you got a party tonight?" a passer-by asked.

Martin replied, "Naw, I'm going to bed early. Whew, I have to go to a *fandango* tommorow at the Furman's. Don't think I can stand another one tonight."

Good, he did have the right man, and he also knew that he would be alone. Slocum waited until the two were down the street before he slunk from the square. He headed back for Nana's. She had gone to work at her sewing job.

He reheated himself some frijoles and wrapped them in

left-over flour tortillas. After his lunch, he went outside and checked the shoes on the bay. They looked secure. He straightened and studied the mountains in the south. Somewhere down there it was warm, even if he had to go deep down to Mexico to find a comfortable temperature. Somewhere down there it was warm and the señoritas danced to good music.

Only twenty dollars left to his name, but he must leave Nana ten of it. The rest and the bay horse should get him to Mexico. But he would need to leave the money and be gone before she returned from work. Be easier to part with her that way. She knew he couldn't stay in Sante Fe— still it was hard to leave her.

He wondered where Chris was. Should be on her way back to Preskitt, maybe the big bear Maggard was with her. Hell, it was Christmas Eve—no time to get all choked up about it.

He closed Nana's door after himself.

The bay tied uphill in the junipers, Slocum watched Martin return home by himself. Then the man came back outside and took a large armful of the firewood stacked by the doorway, looked around, and went back inside.

"Merry Christmas," Slocum said and went to find the horse. So far, Martin hadn't noticed the blasting sticks concealed between some split pieces of firewood already to light in his fireplace.

Slocum rode the stiff horse past the house and down the wash. A hundred yards down the wash, a tumultuous blast struck his back and caused the mustang to suck his tail up his butt.

He checked him, then swung him around to glance back. In the twilight, he could see in the fiery glare the roof debris raining down around the remains of Martin's house. He booted the goosey bay on. One more to even the score for Isaac Denton and Kay. He headed the mustang for the south and crossed the railroad tracks before the Christmas Eve moon rose.

Epilogue

The *El Paso Sun* carried the two-column story about the prominent Santa Fe businessman Ed Martin, killed in a mysterious explosion that leveled his house on Christmas Eve. Under his blanket poncho, Slocum read the article with his back to the adobe wall. A cold wind swept big puffs of dust and old newspapers up the narrow street. Through reading, he went and untied his bay at the hitch rail.

"Still ain't warm enough here," he said, swung up, and reined the pony for the Rio Bravo.

JAKE LOGAN
TODAY'S HOTTEST ACTION WESTERN!

☐ SLOCUM AND THE WOLF HUNT #237	0-515-12413-3/$4.99
☐ SLOCUM AND THE BARONESS #238	0-515-12436-2/$4.99
☐ SLOCUM AND THE COMANCHE PRINCESS #239	0-515-12449-4/$4.99
☐ SLOCUM AND THE LIVE OAK BOYS #240	0-515-12467-2/$4.99
☐ SLOCUM AND THE BIG THREE #241	0-515-12484-2/$4.99
☐ SLOCUM AT SCORPION BEND #242	0-515-12510-5/$4.99
☐ SLOCUM AND THE BUFFALO HUNTER #243	0-515-12518-0/$4.99
☐ SLOCUM AND THE YELLOW ROSE OF TEXAS #244	0-515-12532-6/$4.99
☐ SLOCUM AND THE LADY FROM ABILENE #245	0-515-12555-5/$4.99
☐ SLOCUM GIANT: SLOCUM AND THE THREE WIVES	0-515-12569-5/$5.99
☐ SLOCUM AND THE CATTLE KING #246	0-515-12571-7/$4.99
☐ SLOCUM #247: DEAD MAN'S SPURS	0-515-12613-6/$4.99
☐ SLOCUM #248: SHOWDOWN AT SHILOH	0-515-12659-4/$4.99
☐ SLOCUM AND THE KETCHEM GANG #249	0-515-12686-1/$4.99
☐ SLOCUM AND THE JERSEY LILY #250	0-515-12706-X/$4.99
☐ SLOCUM AND THE GAMBLER'S WOMAN #251	0-515-12733-7/$4.99
☐ SLOCUM AND THE GUNRUNNERS #252	0-515-12754-X/$4.99
☐ SLOCUM AND THE NEBRASKA STORM #253	0-515-12769-8/$4.99
☐ SLOCUM #254: SLOCUM'S CLOSE CALL	0-515-12789-2/$4.99
☐ SLOCUM AND THE UNDERTAKER #255	0-515-12807-4/$4.99
☐ SLOCUM AND THE POMO CHIEF #256	0-515-12838-4/$4.99

Prices slightly higher in Canada

Payable by Visa, MC or AMEX only ($10.00 min.), No cash, checks or COD. Shipping & handling:
US/Can. $2.75 for one book, $1.00 for each add'l book; Int'l $5.00 for one book, $1.00 for each
add'l. Call (800) 788-6262 or (201) 933-9292, fax (201) 896-8569 or mail your orders to:

Penguin Putnam Inc.	Bill my: ☐ Visa ☐ MasterCard ☐ Amex _____(expires)
P.O. Box 12289, Dept. B	Card# _____
Newark, NJ 07101-5289	Signature _____
Please allow 4-6 weeks for delivery.	
Foreign and Canadian delivery 6-8 weeks.	

Bill to:

Name _____

Address _____ City _____

State/ZIP _____ Daytime Phone # _____

Ship to:

Name _____	Book Total	$ _____
Address _____	Applicable Sales Tax	$ _____
City _____	Postage & Handling	$ _____
State/ZIP _____	Total Amount Due	$ _____

This offer subject to change without notice.   Ad # 202 (8/00)